MATE OF HER HEART

MATE OF HER HEART

WILDE CREEK ONE

BY R. E. BUTLER

ISBN: 1494378337
ISBN 13: 9781494378332

Mate of Her Heart
(Wilde Creek One)

By R.E. Butler

License Notes

This ebook is licensed for your personal enjoyment only. This ebook may not be re-sold or given away to other people. If you would like to share this book with another person, please purchase an additional copy for each recipient. If you're reading this book and did not purchase it, or it was not purchased for your use only, then please purchase your own copy. Thank you for respecting the hard work of the author.

Cover by Ramona Lockwood

———·———

I would like to extend sincere thanks to Alexis Arendt at Word Vagabond for editing this story. To the wonderful Amanda

Pederick - thank you not only for beta-reading, but for being a great friend, brain storming queen, and all around fab gal.

To the *Wild Shifter Babes Street Team* - You are amazing!

To my Aunt B. L. my husband, B. B., I love you both.

To my friends and fans, thank you all for your support!

TABLE OF CONTENTS

CHAPTER ONE

One week. That's how much time Eveny Moore had left before her first heat-cycle struck and her body would try to attract a male to impregnate and mate her. She looked at the calendar on the wall of her father's kitchen and touched her stomach through the thin material of her top. A week seemed like both an eternity away and a very short time period. She could do a lot of things in a week. Break a habit. Learn a new song on the guitar. Go on a vacation. But the one thing she couldn't do in a week was tell the one male on earth who meant more to her than anything – her best friend, Luke Elrich – that she wanted to mate with *him*.

He deserved to know. But every time she looked into his big blue eyes and noticed the dimples in his cheeks when he smiled, all her good intentions fled. How had the boy that she'd been stuck to like glue since they were kids turned into such a gorgeous specimen? And why was life so unfair? If life were really fair, he wouldn't have turned into such a hunk with a compassionate personality. He'd have wound up looking like Quasimodo, and she wouldn't be so torn about her biological duty as a wolf shifter. She needed more time. She'd had plenty of time over the last several years to talk to him, of course, but she was a big fat coward and now she was nearly out of time. She could feel her heat-cycle coming on, and knew that at most she had a week before she would be consumed by it.

"Dinner's ready, Eveny," her father called from the back deck.

The warm September Saturday evening had inspired her father to make his famous beer-can chicken, and she'd spent the afternoon

1

peeling and marinating vegetables for the grill pan, which he'd begrudgingly allowed her to place alongside his chicken.

She peeled her eyes away from the calendar and exhaled loudly. She couldn't stop her coming heat-cycle by willing it away. Her whole life, she'd known that she would experience her first heat-cycle during the month of September in her twenty-fifth year. She'd known it as a harsh truth of her werewolf biology. But she hadn't welcomed it. Most of the females in her pack assured her that the heat was all good times and hot sex, but Eveny knew that no matter the good times, or the hot sex, if a male came inside a female during her heat-cycle, he was the one that she was mated to. And for wolf shifters, mated meant married. And married meant *forever*.

Joining her father on the deck, she sat on one of the wrought-iron chairs and lifted her plate. He set a chicken quarter on it and she set it on the table, reaching for the grill pan full of teriyaki-glazed veggies.

After scooping a generous portion onto her plate, she held it across the table and waited for her father to take it.

He wrinkled his nose. "We're wolves, Eveny, not rabbits."

"Last time I checked we're also human, and humans eat a variety of things, including vegetables. And rabbits don't grill their vegetables, the flames singe their fur."

Her father, Dade, smiled warmly and chuckled. "Fine, baby girl," he said, placing a scoop of her medley of snow peas, zucchini, yellow squash, and carrots on his plate.

She pulled the meat from the bones and made a neat pile on her plate, placing the bones on a separate plate. Eating slowly, she considered a hundred ways to start a conversation with her father about her concerns with the coming heat. She wasn't embarrassed to talk about the physical aspects of the heat with her dad – after her mother passed away when she was eleven, her father had become both parents to her and they had no secrets.

Well…one secret.

The secret that was the cause of her balking against the traditions of her people. If she couldn't have Luke, then she didn't want to take a mate. Not this heat-cycle and not for any future heat-cycles. Her beast liked Luke, cared about him, and she loved him and had always loved him. But her people's specist attitudes towards humans kept her from having more than a friendship with Luke. If she chose to go through her heat-cycle with him, knowing that she wouldn't be able to stop herself from making him her mate completely, she'd be kicked out of the pack in shame and any children they had together would be rogues. Rogue wolves weren't welcome in their hometown of Wilde Creek. Pack members were not allowed to associate with rogues. She'd never see her father again. Or her brother, Acksel, the pack alpha.

Shivering as she thought about her brother having to kick her out of the pack and watching people she'd known her entire life turn their backs on her as if she were worthless, she tried to switch her mind to a kinder topic. Except all she could think about was how little time a week was to spend with her best friend before she had to go through her heat-cycle.

"You didn't save me any chicken? What the hell?" Acksel asked, plopping down in the chair next to her. The chair creaked under his weight and she winced, wondering if it would survive the meal.

She elbowed him. "You snooze you lose, bro," she said with a laugh.

He scowled at her. "I got tied up in a council meeting."

"Aw, heavy is the head that wears the crown."

Their father got up and went to the grill, returning with another chicken. Acksel's eyes lit up. Even if he was a badass alpha, he was still a kid at heart. And no one liked their father's beer-can chicken more than Acksel.

"Have some veggies, Acksel," she touched her fork to the edge of the grill pan.

Acksel's wrinkled nose was an exact replica of her father's, and she stifled a giggle.

"I'm not human, Ev. I don't need vegetables and fruits to round out my diet." He took a bite of chicken and stabbed his fork in her direction. "You're no human, either."

Their father had always tolerated her friendship with Luke. He was friendly with the humans who lived in Wilde Creek. But Acksel didn't like humans at all. He had been a scrawny kid and the humans in school had treated him badly. No one treated him badly now, though. He was six-and-a-half feet of muscular, fit male with the enhanced strength and speed of their shifter genes. After he fought and beat the former alpha at twenty-six, no one said Acksel's name without respect.

She let the dig about not being human go and turned her attention to the meal. Acksel and their father talked pack politics. Their father had never been alpha, but Acksel often talked to him about the goings-on in the pack. Their father had served on the council to the former alpha, but as was Acksel's right when he took over, he had disbanded the council and filled it with an entirely new group who he could speak to when decisions needed to be made.

Their father said, "You chose to fight for the position of alpha, Acksel, and I'm certain I don't need to remind you that it's not a position that can be taken lightly. You're the center of influence for the pack. What you say is law, period, which means choosing your words carefully."

Acksel grunted. "You never fought for the position of alpha."

"I didn't want to. It's a big job and requires balancing the needs of the individual pack members with the overall good of the pack." Their father looked at Eveny for a moment and then looked at Acksel. "When the former alpha took over the position, yes I could have gone against him and probably won. But I had your mother to think of, and you were both little. I didn't want to take on a role in the pack that meant that I would be away from the people who mattered most to me, and one where my life would always be on the line with challenges. But don't think for a moment that I don't understand what you went through to become alpha or what you deal with now. I served on the council for many years."

Eveny spoke up. "If you'd been single, would you have wanted to be alpha?"

Their father smiled at her. "Maybe. It does have its perks."

4

Acksel grinned lasciviously and Eveny made a face. She was pretty sure her dad was talking about sex with females as a perk of being alpha, and she didn't want to think about her father — or her brother — in that way.

Their father said, "I'm proud of you, Acksel, and all that you've accomplished at such a young age. But even if you weren't the alpha, I would still be proud of you, because you're my son and I love you."

The meal passed and she was no closer to talking to her father about her concerns than when she'd sat down at the table.

"I'll do the dishes later," her dad said as he put the last of the plates on the counter. Turning to face her, he leaned against the counter and folded his arms. "Why don't you tell me what's bothering you?"

Acksel walked into the kitchen and froze. "Is something wrong?"

"No," she lied. "I've just got some things on my mind."

Acksel cocked his head to the side and raised a brow. At one time, she and her only brother had been very close. But he was very driven to be the biggest and baddest werewolf, and once he'd shifted and began to train with his eye on the alpha position, he'd become less of a friend to her. They weren't strangers by any stretch, but she knew very little about the man he had become. It was moments like this, when he looked at her with brotherly concern, that she missed the friendship they'd shared. "I told Jerry that your heat was coming up and you were to get the time off with pay. Is he giving you a hard time?"

She worked part-time in the office of Ferrity's Construction, a pack-run outfit. Her boss, Jerry, was a friend of her father's, and she'd been working for him since she was sixteen. "No, Jerry is being kind as always."

Her father narrowed his gray eyes at her. "You're worried about the heat?"

She swallowed hard, amazed at how her father always seemed to know what was going on with her. The only thing he had never figured out was how much she cared for Luke. According to her pack's laws, as a female wolf, Eveny was supposed to take a male wolf as her mate during her heat-cycle and further the wolf species by having the first of many pups. It was unacceptable for her to want to mate with a human. And that was aside from the fact that she'd never even talked to Luke about becoming mates in the first place. It wasn't a conversation she could have over the course of a week and expect him to understand fully what it all meant, to make a decision that would affect the rest of his life forever.

Nodding, she clenched her hands together, twisting her fingers. "I'm not ready."

Acksel snorted. "You're twenty-five. You've known about your first heat coming this year forever. What's to be ready about?"

Her father cut his gaze to Acksel and growled lightly. "If she's not ready, son, then she's not ready."

Acksel's lip curled up into a snarl. "There's nothing to be ready for."

Anger flashed through her and she stepped towards her brother. "Fuck you, Acksel. You don't have some trick of nature forcing you into a painful heat for a week with the intent of getting you pregnant and settling on a mate. I haven't dated anyone in months. Do you think I want to get a mate like this?" By the time she finished lashing out at her brother, she was standing toe to toe with him, glaring up at his six-foot-six frame and poking him in his chest.

His eyes flashed to the gold of his wolf and he snarled, grabbing her wrist in his hand. "Watch yourself, she-wolf. You may be my sister, but you will treat me with respect."

Her father slipped between them and leaned back, separating them. "She's emotional right now, Acksel. She means no disrespect."

Acksel huffed and glared at her around their dad. "You don't have a choice. You can't undo biology. My advice is to suck it up. If you won't choose a male to go through the heat with, then I'll choose one for you."

All the blood drained from her face. "Don't you dare!"

This time, Acksel's eyes changed to gold and his fangs elongated. "What did you say?"

6

Her father reached behind and shoved her backwards. "Go to your room, Ev. We'll talk later."

She considered for only a brief moment arguing with her brother about his Neanderthal views on females and their place in the pack, but one look at his sharp fangs and glowing eyes and she knew sticking around was a bad idea. Backing away slowly, she left the kitchen and then darted for the door out to the garage. She had converted the attic space over the garage into an apartment when she was eighteen. It was normal for she-wolves in her pack to live with their parents until they mated, but she'd wanted some independence and had chosen to leave the house but still stay close.

An hour later, while she still paced back and forth in the room, her father knocked on the door and opened it. "He's gone," he announced, coming in and sitting down on the small loveseat in front of the hand-me-down television in the corner. She joined him on the couch, sinking into the deep plush.

"I really messed up. I know better than to talk back to Acksel." She put her head in her hands. It was bad enough she wasn't looking forward to the heat because of a bad case of unrequited love with Luke. She didn't need to add herself to her brother's shit-list, too.

Her dad rubbed her shoulder. "He's your brother. It would be hard for anyone to deal with having a family member suddenly become alpha. And he's having trouble, too, balancing the responsibilities of being alpha with his desire as a brother to keep you safe."

She looked at her dad. "If you tell me he just wants what's best for me I'm going to scream."

He chuckled. "Both of us do, but he's coming from more of a political place. You're one of the few unmated females in the pack, baby girl, and the only one to turn twenty-five this year." He paused and rubbed his fingers along his jaw in thought. "I've overheard some talk in the pack that some of the males are pressuring Acksel to choose a mate for you."

"What?" She was shocked.

"You're the alpha's only sister. Your mate would have an 'in' with the alpha that other males could only dream of. Auro is leaving the pack, which means that the beta position will be up for grabs in a few weeks. The alpha's sister's mate might have an edge."

She frowned. It was one thing to feel like males only wanted to mate her because the scent of an unmated female in heat made them go mental. It was another thing to consider that some of them might only care about what mating her could do for *them.*

Silence settled between her and her dad. She wished she could tell him what was really bothering her. She wished she could tell what his reaction would be if she told him that she wanted Luke to take her through her heat. This one, and all future ones. She just didn't know how he would take the revelation.

Her dad cleared his throat. "You can insist that a male you are with during your heat use condoms. Unless he climaxes inside you, you wouldn't be mated."

She knew that wouldn't work. She'd talked to other females in the pack who had the intention of not mating during their first heat, only to lose their minds to the need sweeping through them. One of the girls she'd gone to school with had turned twenty-five last year, and the male that she'd chosen to go through the heat with had decided to withhold sex from her until she agreed to become his mate. According to Reba, she'd been so mindless with lust and filled with pain from the heat that she thought she would die if she didn't have sex. Things were okay between her and her mate now, but she still harbored some resentment at how he'd tricked her. Eveny didn't want to put herself in that position.

"I don't trust any of the pack males, Dad."

He frowned and exhaled slowly. "What about the cabin?"

"What about it?" Her grandfather had built a cabin about thirty miles north of town, deep in the woods and outside of the pack territory. Her father had taken her and Acksel there in the summer for vacations and in the winter for the holidays.

"You can use it as a safehouse. It's outside of pack territory, so it's not technically under Acksel's jurisdiction. Go there the day before your heat so you don't leave a scent trail, take supplies for the duration, and lock the doors. No one in the pack would think you'd go there. I have to tell you, though, that it's my understanding that trying to handle a heat by yourself is going to be very difficult. You'll be in pain for most of the time."

Hope bloomed inside her. She threw her arms around her dad's neck and hugged him. "Thanks, Dad. I'll take some pain over having to be mated right now."

She stood from the couch, wanting to dance a jig at how relieved she felt. He looked at her in amusement and then sobered quickly. "You can buy yourself a pass for this heat, baby girl, but next year you're going to have to choose a male."

He stood and pecked her cheek, leaving her alone in the apartment. She danced a little bit, letting out a whoop of happiness. A plan formed in her mind and she stopped dancing around the hardwood floors.

I really want Luke, she said to herself. *Even a year from now won't change anything.*

She knew what she would face if she chose a human mate. She'd be outcast. Shunned. Vilified. A "here's what not to do with your life" tale for future generations. If she was honest with herself, she knew that she couldn't take a wolf for a mate, because no matter who he might be, he wouldn't be Luke. Her wolf rumbled in agreement in her mind, and she knew that she would choose him.

But she only had a week, and that wasn't nearly enough time to talk to Luke about a life-altering commitment. It would be unfair of her to spring such a monumental decision on her best friend with so little time to make it. She knew without a doubt that he would help her with this heat, but she didn't just want his help, she wanted him forever. So she would go through this heat by herself, and then she would spend the next year helping Luke to understand the serious commitment she wanted to make with him. She didn't want him to think that she was choosing him just because she wasn't interested in any pack males. Or that she would resent walking away from her pack and family forever because she chose him. She loved him. She didn't think she would ever make a more difficult decision in her life than choosing him over her pack and family, but she would never be happy in a mating with a wolf. And even if she lost her brother and father and her pack, she would gain Luke, who held her heart in his hands. The thought of walking away from her father was like a knife in her chest. She'd lose the one male who had been there for her for her *entire* life, had loved her without question, and accepted everything about her. But for Luke she would do even that most difficult thing.

The question was…would Luke accept her? Knowing what she was going to give up for him? Would he wonder at his own value for her to lose so much? There wasn't a doubt in her mind that he was it for her, no matter the consequences of her actions. It would hurt to never see her family again, or her pack, but facing a lifetime of unhappiness with a male that she didn't love was an alternative that she didn't want to contemplate.

Forgive me, Dad, she thought, as she walked to her closet and removed a suitcase to start packing, brushing tears from her eyes.

CHAPTER TWO

Luke Elrich wiped down the bar and looked around the nearly empty room of Poke's on Tuesday night. He'd been tending bar at Poke's since he was twenty-one. In the beginning, he'd promised himself that he would only work at the bar until he finished his degree in business management, but at twenty-seven, with a finished degree, he was still slinging suds. The owner, Teddy Poke, was retiring from the bar business at the end of the year, and Luke was in a good position to buy the bar. He'd go from tending the bar to running it. And he liked that idea a lot.

At the first of the year he'd have his own business, and instead of renting the apartment above the bar, he'd own it as well. Then he could expand. He could hire a cook to run the kitchen and some servers to handle the food, and turn the bar from a *bar* to a place where people came not only to drink, but to eat and hang out. It was the only bar in Wilde Creek. It was foolish not to have it be everything that it could be.

He'd grown up in Wilde Creek his entire life, part of the human population that lived alongside a werewolf pack which had been in the area for many generations. His best friend, Eveny, was the only sister of the pack alpha, Acksel. Eveny was just two years younger than Luke, and they'd been best friends since they were little.

His parents had died in a car accident when he was seven. He'd moved across town to live with his grandma, who had welcomed him with open arms. Down the street from her small Cape Cod-style home was the Moore home, where Eveny lived with her dad and her brother. One night, Luke had been feeling particularly sad about

11

his family and he'd gone out for a walk. He'd been sitting on a fallen log and looking up at the sky when he heard leaves crunching and turned to see a young girl come out from behind a tree.

"You sad?" she asked, approaching him boldly.

"Yeah."

"'Cause your mom and dad are in heaven?"

The reminder made him even sadder, but he didn't want to cry in front of her. "Yeah."

She joined him on the log, her bare feet swinging back and forth. "I think in heaven that you get to do what you want all day. If I was in heaven, I'd want to eat watermelon and watch television." She looked up at the sky and reached over and took his hand. "You think your momma is watching television?"

He sniffled and smiled, looking up at the stars and picturing his mom and dad doing the things they loved best. "I'll bet she's watching her soaps and my dad is working on an old car."

"You wanna be my friend, Luke?"

"Sure, Eveny."

Her little hand squeezed his tightly and they stared up at the sky until the night turned colder and it was time to head home. He walked her back to her house and her father was standing on the porch waiting.

"Thank you for walking her home," Dade said, taking Eveny's hand. "She said that someone was sad and she had to go make them feel better. I guess she was talking about you."

He shuffled his feet, not wanting to admit to the big werewolf that he was sad. "Yes, sir."

"You're welcome to visit with my daughter, Luke, but make sure that it's during the day from now on."

He lifted his head in surprise and Eveny was grinning. "Thanks, Daddy."

"You're welcome, baby girl. Now off to bed with you both."

Luke said goodbye and headed back to his grandma's. That was just the first time that Eveny had been there for him, and he'd repaid the favor many times over himself. Their friendship had deepened over the last twenty years, but they'd never crossed the line between friends and lovers.

Something was changing between them, though, and he was starting to feel as if their days as friends were numbered. As a human, he was not privy to a lot of what went on in the pack, but he knew that the females tended to get married – or what they called 'mated' – in their early-to-mid twenties. That Eveny was still single at age twenty-five was something that he'd heard a lot about lately at the bar. As a bartender, he was fairly invisible when it came to whispered conversations, and he heard a lot more than people probably thought he did.

It seemed like Eveny was hiding something. They never kept secrets from each other. Well, except for the reason why they had never gotten romantic. They'd come close, but she'd always pulled back and he'd gotten to the point where he tried not to think about it anymore. But the thought of her someday hooking up with a wolf made his gut tighten in worry and his vision go red with anger. He wasn't a wolf, but that didn't mean he wouldn't be a good mate for her. He loved her. He'd always loved her.

He'd always believed that what was on the inside was what mattered, not what was on the outside. But that wasn't the case with wolves. There were humans that hated shifters. When they 'came out of the woods' fifty years ago and began to demand equal rights, there were humans that banded together to form protest groups. There were human-rights lobbyists in Washington, along with wolves' rights. He wasn't sure that he'd ever known any human and wolf to marry, but surely in all the time since they revealed themselves, some wolf somewhere had loved a human and they'd made a go of things.

Like he would love to do with Eveny.

So after all this time, after taking her to both his prom and hers, after visiting each other every weekend while he was in college and talking on the phone every night, he was standing on the cusp of possibly losing her forever.

His gut tightened at the thought. He didn't even know if she felt the same about him. He was too *chicken shit*, as she liked to say, to broach the subject. Scared to death to take that first step and lay his feelings out. He'd always thought that *it would ruin our friendship* excuse for not entering a relationship was bullshit. But if he laid his heart out for Eveny and she shot him down, then it *might* ruin their friendship, and there was a part of him that was not willing to risk the woman who was the most important person in his life.

I might lose her no matter what, he thought.

There were things that he couldn't change. He'd never shift into anything furry. He would never be part of the pack. But he could love her better than anyone else. They were made for each other. No two people on earth were more perfect together than he and Ev.

Before his parents died, he'd been out helping his father in the yard one day when his mom called them in for dinner. "Go grab some flowers from the beds over there, kiddo," his dad suggested. Luke ran over to where the day lilies, daffodils, and daisies filled the flower bed that ran alongside the house. He plucked a bunch of daffodils. His dad said, "Give them to your momma, she'll love them."

They walked up the back porch into the house and Luke handed the flowers to her. She hugged him and thanked him for the flowers, and then he heard her kiss his dad. They washed up and sat at the kitchen table, and she brought over the meal for them. It was meatloaf with mashed potatoes, his dad's favorite.

His mom sat down, and after everyone had helped themselves, he noticed that she hadn't taken any meatloaf. "Why aren't you eating any meatloaf?" he asked, taking a bite.

"I don't like meatloaf," she answered, spooning gravy on the pile of potatoes on her plate.

Luke was confused. "If you don't like meatloaf, then why do you make it?"

She had auburn hair that fell past her shoulders in thick curls, and he remembered that she had leaned forward and one curl slipped over her shoulder. "Your dad loves meatloaf, so I make it for him."

Luke was still confused, so he looked at his dad, who smiled broadly and winked. "Someday, son, you'll marry a woman who will cook you things she doesn't like because she loves you."

Luke had thought that sounded like a good thing. Sometime later, after he and Eveny had become best friends, they'd been sitting in the school cafeteria together and he noticed that she'd picked up a cup of fruit cocktail. She didn't like fruit cocktail, because even if she didn't pick the cup with the cherry in it, she swore that all the fruit tasted like cherries and she absolutely hated them. He was surprised to see that not only had she picked up a cup, but she'd gotten one with a cherry on top.

She leaned across the table and put the cup on his tray and smiled at him.

"What are you doing?" he asked.

She shrugged and picked up her fork. "You like that stuff."

"But you don't."

She wrinkled her nose as she looked at it. "Nope. But *you* do."

"Thanks, Ev."

She rolled her eyes but smiled broadly. "It's just fruit, Luke, don't have a cow."

"I won't. I just think you're nice."

It was that day that he'd first started to think of Eveny as more than just his friend. Or at least that perhaps someday they might become more than friends. But neither of them had ever moved forward. There had been times, when they'd been at the movies, or watching TV on the couch, or even when she'd fallen asleep with her head in his lap, that he had ached to touch her and hold her. Be *more* to her than he was. But he'd been scared, and now he felt like a noose was tightening around his neck.

He didn't know what would happen to him if he lost Eveny, but he knew that it would be a dark spot in his soul forever.

"I can't take that chance," he said.

"What?" Henry, one of the regulars, asked, looking up from his beer.

Luke began to wipe down the bar. "Just thinking out loud, Henry. You need a refill?"

Determination filled him. He would not go down without a fight. If Eveny needed to mate someone, why couldn't it be him? If he lost her without even throwing his hat into the ring, then he had no one to blame but himself. Eveny never cared that he was human, and he didn't care that she was a wolf.

He just needed to step out onto the ledge and hope that she would be there with him. If not, then he could at least say he tried. And he'd rather try and lose her, than never try and never know.

CHAPTER THREE

Eveny looked at the impossibly high stack of paperwork that her boss, Jerry, had just laid on her desk. She couldn't even see the man behind it. "Jerry?" she asked, leaning to the side and looking at him.

"You're leaving in a few days and will be gone for a week. I really want to get some of this stuff taken care of before then. I can't pay you vacation time because you're not full-time, but I can pay you for whatever extra hours you work this week so you won't miss the missing paycheck."

"Did my dad put you up to this?" she asked suspiciously. It sounded like something her dad would do – ask his friend to help her out financially even though she hardly had any bills at all. Just her car payment, cable, and cell bills, and whatever incidentals she had.

Jerry quirked his brow. "Don't know what you're talking about, Eveny. Now get to entering all that into the computer. When you're done with this stack, they get filed by date in the tall filing cabinet in the storage room."

She didn't press him about whether her father was instrumental in the extra hours. She was glad for them, regardless of whether it was Jerry's idea or not. Pulling the first page down from the stack, she looked at the old customer order, and began to enter it into the computer. Jerry had just recently upgraded the computers in the tiny office and started doing more things digitally. Part of the reason, she assumed, was because he was running out of space in his filing cabinets. She didn't mind. Busy work would keep her hands moving but her mind free to figure out what to do about her coming heat and Luke.

By the time she was done working for the day, her fingers ached from typing, her back was in knots from sitting in the chair for so long, and her eyes hurt from staring at the computer. "You got a lot done today, Eveny," Jerry said as he walked her out to her car. "I think by the time you take off, you'll have really made a dent in what needs to be done."

"Goodnight, Jerry," she said, not enjoying the thought of another brutal day in front of the computer.

Luke was already at work, and she never called him when he was working unless it was an emergency. Like the time she swerved to avoid hitting a squirrel and smacked the front of her car into a guardrail. He worked at the bar until closing five nights a week.

She promised herself that she would call him tomorrow morning.

But the next day, Acksel woke her up early and asked her to join him for breakfast at Luna's, a tiny diner in town. She couldn't remember the last time that Acksel had asked her to breakfast, so she went, promising herself that she would call Luke at her earliest opportunity.

But that opportunity didn't come that day, either. Or the next. They texted each other, because it turned out that he was extra busy at work, too. She couldn't explain about her heat through texts. And she definitely couldn't tell him that she wanted him to be her mate. She needed to talk to him. But the universe was conspiring against them.

As the time for her to head to the cabin drew closer and closer, she decided that she'd have to save the conversation between them for after she got back from her heat. He would understand how she'd gotten swamped at work. Between Acksel's sudden need to have breakfast with her every day, Jerry's never-ending stack of paperwork, and her utter exhaustion at the end of each day, he would forgive her for not having a chance to explain about the heat before she left.

She definitely wouldn't have told him about wanting to be mates before she left. He'd want to *really* talk. And she would feel compelled to spill all her secrets. It wasn't that she didn't think he felt the same way about her, because she could tell that he cared for her. She just didn't want to have to get into all the nitty-gritty about choosing him and leaving the pack. More than what she would lose, was that he most definitely would have to reconsider buying the bar. If she left the pack, then anyone associated with her – even her mate – was considered *persona non grata* with the pack, and they wouldn't use the bar if he owned it. So she wasn't the only one losing something.

She could feel the heat coming on. It was part of being a female, a gift of sorts, from whoever was in charge of werewolf heats. She could tell to the day when her heat was going to start, and had known for several weeks when the time would come. Now, she knew that at some point tomorrow she would start to feel pressure inside her body and the need to have sex and create a life would soon overwhelm her. Without letting a male come inside her, she would suffer through the entire heat-cycle, which lasted seven days. The only way to shorten a heat-cycle was if she became pregnant before it had run its course. If a male used condoms the whole time, or if the female handled it herself, then it wouldn't ease the number of days. One female in her pack was out of her heat the first day. Another went almost six days.

She had said goodbye to Jerry the night before and promised to let him know when she was back in town. Acksel had woken her up for breakfast once more that morning; this time her father was with him, and they talked at the house instead of going to Luna's.

"Are you sure about this?" Acksel asked with a scowl. "You could trust one of our pack males to take you through the heat without coming inside you."

She returned his scowl with one of her own. "It's so easy for you to make that statement, Acksel. You think because you're honorable that all the males in the pack are, too. It's my body and I should be able to handle my heat the way I want to."

She had kind of hoped that her dad wouldn't tell Acksel about her plans until after she was gone, but that hadn't happened. Now she was staring across the kitchen table at her angry older brother. After her father came to her defense again, Acksel seemed to calm down.

"I'll let it go this time, Eveny. But only once."

She opened her mouth to tell him that he couldn't control when she had a baby or chose a mate and to go fuck himself with a long pole, but she thought better of it. If she pissed Acksel off, he might use his authority as alpha to force her to mate with a male of his choosing this time around. She had a feeling that he'd pick one of his buddies. Mack or Greg. Or Vince.

She shivered inwardly. None of those Neanderthals would make a good mate for her. They'd expect her to take care of them and pop out babies. She'd be metaphorically chained between the kitchen and the bedroom, never free to do what she wanted or make her own choices again.

It strengthened her resolve to speak to Luke after the heat. He was perfect for her. He would love her and let her be a partner in their marriage. And she'd be happy to pop out a bunch of his babies. Little boys and girls with his sapphire blue eyes and dark blond hair.

Her heart warmed. She should have told him months ago that she loved him as more than a friend and let the chips fall where they might. Now she was out of time.

After helping with the dishes, she said goodbye to her dad and brother and went up to her apartment to finish packing. She'd already done the main suitcase. She didn't anticipate needing many clothes, so she had mostly packed her thin, lightweight pajama sets and her bubble bath so she could soak away some of the aches. After making the decision to go through the heat alone, she'd sought the advice of some of her father's female friends who had been through many heats, and they had told her that hot baths would help, but that nothing made the heat go away earlier than seven days except getting pregnant.

She'd been shopping online earlier in the week and had a large package delivered by overnight mail, which had arrived yesterday. From an adult novelty website, she ordered several vibrators and other toys, and had picked up a supply of batteries.

Putting her suitcase by the door, she picked up her cell and contemplated calling Luke, but then she decided to just stop by the bar and say goodbye on the way out of town. She would tell him she was going on vacation and that she wanted to talk to him when she got back.

Feeling like she had things settled, and excited to see him after almost a week apart, she picked up a cooler and carried it to the freezer. She loaded it with frozen steaks and emptied all the ice from the bin and several freezer packs into it before closing the lid. She wouldn't want to cook, but her body would crave meat, and it would be easier to toss a steak onto a pan on the stove than worry about trying to make a complete meal. The refrigerator at the cabin would need a few hours before it was cold enough to keep the meat fresh, so using the cooler for the first day was the best idea.

She put the cooler by the front door, went into her bedroom, and picked up the box of sex toys and batteries and carried it out of the room, with her favorite pillow on top.

She heard a single knock and the front door swung open. She froze as she saw Luke standing there in the doorway, the morning sunlight accentuating the golden hue of his skin. He was a weight-lifter and boxed in his spare time, and the sun seemed to caress his broad shoulders and highlight the tautness of the t-shirt that stretched across his chest. Her mouth watered as she let her eyes roam quickly down his body before her eyes snapped up to meet his.

Luke was here.

And she wasn't ready to talk to him.

Well, her body was. But her brain had stalled out.

What the hell was she going to say?

CHAPTER FOUR

Luke opened the door to Eveny's apartment after knocking once. He frowned when he saw a small suitcase just off to the side, along with a cooler.

"Oh!" Eveny came from the hall carrying a box and a pillow, stopping short when she saw him. She stared at him as if she had never really seen him before. Her eyes flitted up and down his body before meeting his again.

"What's going on, Ev?" he asked, shutting the door and leaning against it. Unhappiness settled over him.

She sank her top teeth into her bottom lip and shifted from foot to foot. "I'm going away for a while."

Surprise shook him. "You're leaving town without saying goodbye?"

Shaking her head, she said, "No, I was going to stop by your place and say goodbye."

"Where are you going?"

"Away," she said, her voice tinged with guilt.

His suspicions were confirmed. "It's your heat, right? You're going into heat."

Her mouth dropped open and her head cocked to the side. "How did you know?"

"I'm not stupid, Ev. I've grown up in the same town with a wolf pack. I don't know everything, but I do know *some* things. At some point, every female disappears." He didn't want to say it, but it tumbled from his lips before he could stop it. "And they almost always come back with a mate."

Her eyes widened. He wanted to be mad at her for thinking he was an idiot, but he wasn't. He was just incredibly sad.

He closed the distance between them and took the box from her hands, putting it on the counter. The lid was closed and it felt heavy, but he didn't know what it contained.

He put his hands on her shoulders as his heart pounded in his chest. "Are you done with me, Ev? Are we not friends anymore?"

She reared back like he'd struck her and tears sprang into her eyes. "No, Luke, never!" Her bottom lip trembled and she stood still for only a moment and then threw herself into his arms.

"I'm going through my heat alone, Luke. My dad is letting me stay in the family cabin for the duration."

He inhaled the sweet scent of her coconut body wash and his body tightened. He tried to clear his thoughts, but all he wanted to do was push her to the floor and fuck her brains out. Make her promise never to leave. "The one in the woods outside of town?"

"Yeah." She looked up at him, her hands twisting in the back of his shirt.

He looked down into her beautiful face and her soft, gray eyes. "Why didn't you say anything before today?"

She swallowed hard. "I wanted to tell you all week. But Jerry kept me busier than usual, Acksel wanted to have breakfast every day before work, and you were working longer hours at the bar. I couldn't tell you about my heat over texts. I was afraid if I told you by text that you'd want to talk in person, and I wasn't ready to answer your questions."

He brushed the hair away from her face and kissed her forehead. "You're still not," he guessed. Eveny had a particular way of doing things, and if someone tried to rush her, she would get flustered and angry.

She shook her head and a tear escaped from the corner of her eye. He brushed it with his thumb. "You can tell me anything, Ev, you know that, right?"

She nodded and he wrapped his arms around her and pulled her close. She sighed deeply and hugged her arms around his waist.

"When I get back, can we talk?"

"We can talk now, sweetheart."

"I don't have time," she whispered, her voice cracking with emotion. "I'm such an idiot."

"Never," he promised, running his hands up and down her back. Something was changing between them right now. They'd hugged before. Kissed, even. Comforted each other in many different ways. But this – holding her in his arms while she struggled with her emotions – seemed intimate in an entirely different way.

He settled his cheek on the top of her head and held her. "I'm here, Ev. I'm not going anywhere unless you tell me otherwise."

A shiver wracked her body and she took in a shaky breath. Looking up at him with tears pooling in her eyes, she said, "You're my best friend, Luke. I don't want you to go anywhere."

"Then I won't," he promised. And he'd keep that promise. Until she told him to take a hike, he'd stand by her side through anything.

"I'll be gone a week," she said, hugging him a little tighter and then stepping away. Wiping under her eyes with shaking fingers, she gave him a watery smile. "I'll come find you and we'll talk. Okay? I'll tell you everything, I swear."

"If you need me, you can call me anytime and I'll come up to the cabin."

"I know you will." She paused with her hand on the front door. "I love you, Luke. You know that, right?"

His heart pounded with joy. He kissed her on the lips. "I know you do, Ev. I love you, too."

He helped her carry her things to her car and when she was packed up, they said goodbye and he followed her in his truck as they pulled away from her dad's house. He followed her through town and then turned towards the bar as she headed north. As he drew closer to the bar, he considered turning around and following her up to the cabin, but if she wanted him there, then she would have asked him. Right?

The truth was he didn't have any idea what she was going to go through with her heat. Maybe just getting out of town was all she needed. He climbed the stairs to his apartment two at a time and decided to call his grandma. He made it a point to check in with her at least once a week. The spry old girl was always out with her friends, playing Mah Jong or doing yoga. She even brought her friends in to the bar once a month to have drinks.

"Are you making me any grandbabies yet?" she asked when he said hello.

He chuckled. She had been asking him that question at least once a week for the last several years. If things were actually changing between him and Eveny, then maybe it wasn't all that far off. The thought of Eveny's belly stretched out with his child made him feel practically giddy. A little girl with her brown hair, gray eyes, and tender heart.

"I'm working on it, Grams."

"Oh? Anyone I know?"

His grandma liked to gossip, but she would keep anything he said between them because, as she liked to say, 'you don't gossip about family'. "I think Eveny and I might be starting something."

There was a significant pause and he felt unhappiness settle into his gut. "What's wrong?"

She hummed in her throat. "My friend Vera is a wolf and she's friends with Eveny's father. She told me last night while we were playing Mah Jong that Eveny was disappearing for her heat-cycle so she didn't have to take a mate. Dade's not too happy about it, but he'd walk on hot coals for his daughter."

"Ev told me as much."

"Do you know what the heat-cycle is?"

"No."

"Well, from what Vera told me, every she-wolf goes into heat during the fall of her twenty-fifth year and every fall after unless she's pregnant or nursing. The heat makes the she-wolves crazy for *relations*, and if a she-wolf is with a male wolf during her heat, she'll most likely become pregnant and they'll become mates."

His brain stalled out. "I didn't know that, Grams."

"Of course you didn't, honey, we're humans. Wolves keep to their own kind. Vera said that it's nearly impossible for a female to go through the heat on her own, but that Eveny's father was going to let her try to tough it out this year. Next year, though, if she hasn't chosen a mate to go through the heat with, her brother is going to pick one for her. And you know what that will mean."

He did know. If Acksel chose a male for Eveny, then Luke would lose her forever.

"She seems certain she can get through the heat, Grams. She said she wants to talk when she gets back."

He could hear her smile in her voice. "I'm glad, Luke. You're a good man and you've been waiting for that girl for a long time."

He wasn't working at the bar that night, so he headed out to food shop, then picked up a sandwich from the deli and caught up on his favorite police drama. Eveny texted him before she arrived at the cabin and told him that the cell reception was spotty and that he shouldn't worry if he didn't hear from her. She signed off with an XOXO, and he grinned. Something was definitely changing between them.

He worked the following night and his mind drifted to Eveny again and again. He hadn't slept well the night before. Every time he closed his eyes, he wondered what she was doing in the cabin by herself and he wished he was there with her. He wondered why she had chosen to go alone instead of asking him to come with her.

Someone snapped their fingers in front of his face and he snapped back from his thoughts to see Teddy leaning across the bar. Just then the front door opened and Eveny's brother, Acksel, strode in ahead of a group of pack members.

"Hey, Teddy. What can I do for you?"

"You can head home for the night."

He glanced at his watch. "I've still got three hours on my shift."

"Pack meeting," Teddy said, jerking his head towards the back of the bar where the wolves were gathering. A steady stream of men were now walking through the bar, and the sound of tables being moved around filled the room. The pack that ran in Wilde Creek had about one hundred members, and all were accountable to Acksel as alpha. It seemed like the alpha was a mixture of king and boss and father all rolled into one.

"Sure," Luke nodded. "I'll see you tomorrow."

Teddy wasn't pack either, but he had a long-standing relationship with them, and Acksel always did pack business in the bar. Except for what Eveny called *council meetings*, which he held at his own home. When Luke took over the bar, he'd have to have a conversation with Acksel about the pack. He would be a fool to say anything to make Acksel take his pack away from the bar, and he wanted to make sure that Acksel knew that the wolves were always welcome.

And of course, in his perfect world, Eveny wouldn't be doing office work part-time with the construction crew, but working with him at the bar. In the back, of course, where he could keep her away from prying eyes. If it really was his perfect world, she wouldn't be working at all; she'd be too busy trying to catch up on sleep from their active sex life.

He left the bar and went into the back office and clocked out, heading out the back door. To the left of the back door was a set of metal steps that went up to the two-bedroom attic apartment that he'd lived in since he was twenty-one. He opened the door and walked in, shutting and locking it behind him. The ceiling fan swirled overhead. He left it on constantly because it tended to get really warm in the attic during the daytime when the sun shone, even in the winter.

He'd skipped dinner during the evening rush, and he rummaged in the refrigerator and made himself a sandwich. Turning on the TV, he flipped stations long enough to realize that there wasn't anything worthwhile to watch, and turned it off. It was then that he heard the rumble of engines as cars left the parking lot. A familiar voice drifted up through the open window, and he crept to the window so he could listen without being seen. He didn't make a habit of eavesdropping, but something about the hushed conversation stirred his curiosity. Especially once he heard Eveny's name.

—— · ——

Acksel sat in the center of the corner booth at Poke's and waited while his top-ranked men filed into the bar, moved tables and chairs around, and prepared for the meeting. Once a week he got together with the highest-ranked males and discussed pack business. He watched with a snarl on his lips as the human that his sister was friends with exited the bar. Luke was dangerous. Dangerous to their pack's way of life. Dangerous to Eveny.

The seventeen males settled quickly and Teddy, the bar owner, dropped off pitchers of draft beer and enough mugs for everyone, then scuttled away into the back office after making sure that the bar was empty of humans and the front door was locked.

Acksel had only been alpha for a few years, but he kept a tight leash on his people. If anyone got out of line, he knocked them on their ass. He'd clawed his way to the top leaving a trail of broken bones, concussions, and blood in his wake, and he would do anything to keep his seat of power.

Even if it meant taking away his sister's choices from her.

His wolf growled in protest in his mind but he muzzled the beast and ignored the ache in his heart. Eveny couldn't see the forest for the trees. She thought she could bide her time and wait out the heat this cycle, but she didn't see how restless the males were becoming in the pack. If his father hadn't intervened, he would have forced her to take a male this heat.

His thoughts drifted to the human, Luke, again, and his fangs elongated in rage. Eveny might think she was being secretive, but Acksel could read her like a book. She'd been in love with that fucking human since she was a kid and her protests of "I'm not ready to take a mate" were just her trying to plan a way to take the human as her mate. Which Acksel could not allow. He'd been worried that she might try to ask him to come along with her to the cabin, so he'd spoken to Teddy and asked him to keep Luke busy at the bar. And then he'd gone to Eveny's boss, Jerry, and had him saddle her with lots of busywork and extra hours. Adding in Acksel's *let's hang out* breakfasts all week, he knew that she hadn't had time to have a real conversation with Luke. But that wouldn't last forever.

As his only sister, she held a place of reverence in the pack. Her mate would be his brother in the pack and brother-in-law in the human world. If she chose a human as her mate, then she was turning her back not only on the pack but on him and his father. Her taking a human as a mate would be seen as a weakness on Acksel's part to ensure that his family line remained pure. His alpha status could be called into question. He'd have to answer challenges and fight to prove his worth as alpha. He'd do it, but he didn't want to have to. He wanted Eveny to toe the line and do what was expected of her. Namely, to take a worthy male as a mate, not some pathetic human.

If she did manage to take the human for her mate, Acksel would be forced to mark her as a rogue, slashing his claws across her arm as a warning to other packs that she couldn't be trusted. He and his dad would lose her. It would be as if she were dead, but she would be very much alive. He couldn't do that to his dad, and he couldn't do it to himself.

In spite of promising his father that he would let her go through the heat on her own, he had his own plans. He was sure that she was already in the throes of the heat and she would thank him later for sending a male to relieve her. He just had to choose the right male.

He rapped his knuckles on the worn tabletop and the wolves quieted. "Auro, let's hear the minutes of the last meeting."

Auro was his beta, the wolf who had fought to become second-in-command. He was just a few years older and mated to a she-wolf pregnant with their first child. Her father had taken ill after getting injured during a full moon hunt, and they were leaving the Wilde Creek pack and heading to her home pack so she could care for him. The September full moon would be his last as beta and then Acksel would have to hold rank fights to determine who would take over. He wasn't looking forward to it. He liked the pack the way it was now. He was a very *status quo* sort of guy. If it's not broken, don't fucking touch it.

Auro opened the notes program on his phone and read off the minutes from last week's meeting, and then Acksel discussed the few issues that were still outstanding, ending with the prep for the rank fights.

"Preliminary fights will begin at three p.m. on the twenty-third, two days after the full moon. Only males and mated females can attend. The location is to be determined at a later point, but will most likely be behind my home. Questions?"

Dean, a wolf a few years younger than him, said, "We want to talk about your sister." A chorus of agreement drifted from the group.

His hackles rose immediately and he let his wolf loose enough to allow his eyes to change color and his fangs to elongate. Rising from his seat, he snarled loudly and everyone went quiet. "My sister is my responsibility and is off-limits. Am I clear?"

He glared at the members of his pack and growled for effect. All eyes dropped to the floor. If anyone had met his eyes, he would have taken it as a challenge to his authority and kicked their ass. Being alpha meant he had to constantly prove that he was worthy of the position.

After a few more moments of silence, he sat back and willed his beast to settle. He knew that if anyone had the stones to come after him, they'd do it in public so they could be assured of becoming the next alpha. *If* that male could beat him, which was doubtful. Acksel hadn't become alpha because he had a winning personality.

Returning to the original topic, he informed the males that any who wished to challenge for beta had to fight in the preliminaries or they would be disqualified. He opened the floor to issues, and when there were none, he dismissed the wolves. Most stayed put, drinking their beers and talking, but some headed off.

Leaning back, he looked around at the males and ticked off their attributes in his mind. *Too old. Too young. Raging jackass.* He reminded himself that although the intention was to choose a male for Eveny to go through the heat with *only*, he was well aware that things happened. Condoms broke. Or were not used at all. Deep down, his wolf lamented what he was planning to do to Eveny, but judging from a few secretive looks from several males that he'd beaten out for the position for alpha, he knew that if Eveny didn't take a mate this heat, she could be used against him to get him to step down.

I'm protecting her, he argued with his wolf. *It's for her own damn good.*

Bullshit.

Shaking his head, he cleared his thoughts and shoved the guilt way down in his gut. He'd make it up to her somehow. And she'd eventually forgive him once she understood that he'd done it for her own good.

An hour later, most of the males were calling it a night. "Vince." Acksel called the male who was third-ranked in the pack. As theto, he had a lot of responsibility, and he was well known in the pack for being a no-nonsense male. At almost thirty-three, he was older than Eveny by eight years, but he was foreman at the construction company and owned his own home. Vince had supported Acksel in his desire to become Alpha. He was loyal and dedicated to the pack, voicing his concerns about making changes to long-held traditions. And no one would mess with Eveny with Vince by her side.

Does she even like him?

"I need to speak to you privately. Outside." Acksel stood and moved out of the booth and Vince followed him through the back and out into the parking lot.

Vince Corelli leaned against the steel door and hooked his thumbs in his pockets. "Something up, Acksel?"

For a heartbeat, Acksel almost kept his mouth shut and dismissed Vince, but he forged ahead.

Keeping his voice low, Acksel said, "I want you to do me a favor, Vince."

"Name it," Vince said.

Exhaling quickly, Acksel said, "Eveny has chosen to go through her heat alone. I don't think she understands what she's going to go through, and she's alone with no way to contact anyone for help."

Vince's brows rose in surprise. "You're asking me to take Eveny through her heat?"

Acksel nodded. "Use condoms unless she says otherwise."

His eyes narrowed but he didn't say anything.

Acksel gritted his teeth until his jaw ached. "Eveny needs help, Vince. You're one of the front-runners for beta, and I know that you'll treat my sister with respect in *all* ways."

Vince nodded and extended his hand. Acksel gripped it. "Thank you for trusting me, Acksel."

A lump formed in Acksel's throat as he told Vince how to find the cabin where Eveny was staying. As he walked back into the bar to say goodnight to Teddy, he nearly told Vince not to go, but he reminded himself that he was doing it for Eveny's protection. She might not want to be mated right now, but Vince would take good care of her and eventually she'd forgive Acksel and love Vince.

Doubt and worry settled over him, but he shuttered the feelings away and headed home. It was done now. He'd sealed Eveny's fate. Unless Vince refrained from coming inside her, Eveny would have a mate in a week or less, and possibly be pregnant.

Forgive me, sis.

———

Fury stole through Luke as he listened to Acksel give Eveny away as if she were a piece of furniture and not a person. He pulled his cell from his back pocket and dialed Eveny's number once Acksel had gone back into the bar. He had to warn her.

The phone went directly to voicemail. He didn't know if that meant she had it turned off or if she didn't have service. "Ev," he whispered, "Acksel is sending Vince Corelli up to the cabin to take you through your heat. Get out of there and call me."

He heard the beeping of cell phone buttons being pressed and he froze, listening.

"Hey, you busy?" Vince asked to whoever he had called. "You know the alpha's little she-bitch sister? Guess what our *king* just asked me to do?"

Rage blinded him, turning his vision red and making his blood boil, as he listened to Vince repeat Acksel's request as he walked towards his vehicle in the back parking lot. Luke had to strain to hear the rest of the conversation, but one sentence told him everything he needed to know. "Grab Rufus and Barry and meet me at my place in five."

Luke knew from the tone in Vince's voice that he didn't have any good intentions when it came to Eveny. She was unprotected and virtually helpless right now, by her own brother's hand. Eveny was stronger than a human thanks to her werewolf strength, but she couldn't hope to go up against four horny males intent on raping her.

He snapped into action and packed a bag with clothes and toiletries quickly, just in case he survived, and grabbed a second bag, leaving it empty. He boxed in his spare time and lifted weights. He could take on one wolf. Maybe two. But not four. And Vince was a vicious fighter in his human form. If the males shifted into their wolf forms then Luke was as good as dead. But he didn't care about that. The only thing that mattered was giving Eveny enough time to escape. If he died in the process, at least he would know that she was safe.

He left his apartment and opened the back door to the bar. He could hear some sounds from inside the bar, which told him that some of the wolves were still there. For a moment he considered finding Acksel and telling him what was going on, but he knew that Acksel would never believe him. Acksel detested humans, and he'd always hated Luke's friendship with Eveny. If he tried to tell Acksel that one of his wolves was arranging a gang-rape of Eveny, Acksel would most likely not believe him and then beat him all to hell. And that would leave Eveny defenseless.

He walked past the office and into one of the storage rooms where Teddy kept some items that most people in the bar didn't know about. Sometimes, wolves caused trouble, and if Acksel wasn't in the bar to keep a lid on things, then it was only Teddy and Luke. Opening a storage locker, Luke filled up the bag with two stun batons, two canisters of pepper spray, and an aluminum baseball bat. After some consideration, he shoved some flares into the bag, too.

He had seen Teddy use the stun baton on a rowdy wolf when Luke first started tending bar. Even with the wolf's enhanced strength, he still hit the ground when Teddy zapped him and made him think twice about acting up in the bar again.

The best option would be for Luke to get to Eveny first and get her out of the cabin, into his truck, and safely on the way home before Vince and his buddies showed up. He didn't believe in luck, but Luke sure hoped to fuck that luck was on his side as he raced out of the bar and jumped into his truck, slamming his foot onto the gas and roaring out of the parking lot like the devil was on his tail.

But it wasn't his tail that he was worried about it. It was Ev's. If anyone laid a hand on her, he'd never forgive himself.

CHAPTER FIVE

When Eveny saw Luke's truck turn off towards the bar, she almost turned around and followed him. Doing that, though, would mean seeing him again, and she wasn't sure she could keep her hands off him if she did. The heat was almost upon her, and the desire to touch and hold someone was already creeping into her subconscious. But more than that, she was feeling unsure of her decision to go things alone and she knew that Luke would help her in a heartbeat. With one word, he'd take her to the cabin and do whatever she needed. Then she'd be making love to her best friend and they'd end up mated and she'd be pregnant within a week. Which was all fine and good for her, but she couldn't saddle Luke with that without a thorough discussion.

Which was why leaving and being alone was best. When the heat was over, she'd tell him everything about what being a human mated to a werewolf meant, not only for her, but for him.

Not for the first time in her life, she cursed being a wolf shifter. Although she loved prowling and hunting in her wolf form, she hated the shifting process, which cracked and shifted bones around in her body and hurt more often than not. She hated the hierarchy bullshit that meant that, as alpha, Acksel was in control of her destiny and would kick her out of the pack - and her family - for being with the man that she loved.

By the time she got to the cabin and parked around back, she knew that waiting out the heat and then talking to Luke about mating with her was the right thing to do. She would even make a list of the pros and cons for him so that he could see what they both had the potential to gain and lose with the mating. She never wanted him to say that she hadn't told him everything. If he walked away because it was too much for him, she still wouldn't want to mate with a wolf, but she had a feeling that Acksel would push her during next year's heat-cycle and she'd end up mated. But that would be a mate only in title. Luke was the mate of her heart. Her perfect match.

After filling up the generator with gasoline that she had brought along in two ten-gallon containers, she turned it on and then unlocked the back door. There was no central air conditioning in the cabin, but it was cool enough in the evenings to not need it, and there were several ceiling fans, plus rectangular fans to be placed in the windows. And if she needed it, there was a small window air conditioner that she could use.

It was lunchtime, and her stomach rumbled, but she wanted to get settled first before she ate. The cabin was one large room; a small bathroom and closet lined the back wall, next to a door which led out onto a small back porch. The generator ran the water heater, and the running water in the cabin was collected with a cistern, so she would have fresh drinking water and hot water for her baths. The main room of the cabin was separated into three areas: eating, sleeping, and sitting. A worn-out couch faced a picture window that overlooked one section of the woods. Her father always said that nature was the best television show ever invented. When they'd come to stay when she was younger, he would drink his coffee on the couch and watch out the window for hours. A wood-burning stove sat in the corner, and she had many fond memories of watching her dad fill up the stove and warm up the house when they came during the winter holidays.

The kitchen was compact and efficient, furnished with a butcher block table and three chairs, a long counter with a sink, a small refrigerator, and a two-burner stove. There was a charcoal grill in the small storage shed out back, but she didn't plan to go to that much trouble to cook.

The sleeping area held an unmade king-sized bed with a frame made of twisted branches that had been stripped and sanded smooth so that the white of the trunk showed through in places where the bark had been scratched away. A matching table stood next to the bed and held a battery-operated alarm clock which appeared to be dead. She didn't need the clock. Her body would tell her when the heat was over and the time of day didn't really matter when she could look outside and judge whether it was morning or afternoon or evening. Turning in a slow circle, she looked at the four walls that were going to be her home for the duration of her heat, and took in a deep breath. This was part of her family's heritage, a place of safety where she'd made many wonderful memories with her family.

She remembered her mother standing in the kitchen in one of her father's oversized shirts, making eggs and bacon. Eveny and Acksel had slept on air mattresses on the floor and she always fell asleep to the sound of her parents' muffled conversations. She realized she didn't talk about her mom with anyone but Luke. He'd understood the devastation of losing a parent, because he'd lost both. He had been there for her, let her cry, and listened to anything she wanted to say while she'd grieved. He'd been her rock. And he still was.

Pressing her hand to her abdomen, she decided that when she and Luke had a girl, she'd like to name her after her mother - Miriam. She knew that Luke would like that. And she'd want to name two more of their kids after his parents, Rebecca and Paul. And his grandma, Louise. And her dad, Dade. Chuckling to herself, she wondered if Luke would mind having that many kids.

Thinking about her dad made her heart ache in a bad way. She didn't want to lose him. But she wouldn't lose him *yet*. Until she and Luke mated officially, she would still be able to spend time with him, and she'd just make the most of it.

If Luke wanted to be her mate.

She smiled. She couldn't think of a scenario in which Luke would say no to her.

After checking out the small bathroom, with its tub, sink, and toilet, she returned to the car and brought in the cooler and the box. Leaving a steak out on the counter to thaw, she closed the lid on the cooler and opened the box. They didn't keep linens in the cabin, so she had brought a set of sheets and towels. She made the bed, laying her pillow against the headboard and smoothing her hands down the sheets. When she'd known she was coming up to the cabin, she'd foregone using the inexpensive sheets that her dad kept to bring up here, choosing instead to invest in a set of high thread-count sheets in a butter-yellow color. The sheets were smooth under her fingers, almost like silk but heavier.

She bustled around, cleaning the bathroom so it was free of dust and spider webs, removing the dust cover on the couch, and opening the windows and setting the fans inside to air out the musty smell. The day passed quickly as she prepared to settle in for the next week. She decided to turn in early that night. Although she was feeling perfectly normal, she expected the heat to come upon her at some point during the next day, and she knew that sleep would be hard to come by.

Changing into a pair of pajama shorts and a cami, she turned off the overhead light and climbed into bed. The cabin was dark, and she closed her eyes and settled under the sheet. Her hand brushed over the empty space next to her and she wished that Luke was there with her. As she drifted off to sleep, he was the last thing on her mind.

———·———

Eveny woke up at dawn, drenched in sweat with her stomach cramping. The sheet was twisted around her body and at some point she'd pulled off her pajamas and tossed them on the floor. Her hands trembled as she untangled herself from the sheet. She rolled onto her side with a groan, pressing her hand into her stomach. She was burning up. In pain. And the only thing she could think of was that she should have asked Luke to come with her. It was bad already, and she'd only been awake for a few minutes. She had seven days of this.

Slipping from the bed, she went into the bathroom and wet a washcloth, pressing it onto her face and neck to try to cool down.

She drank several glasses of cold water and then stumbled back to the bed and lifted the box from the floor.

When she'd been shopping online for sex toys, she'd only bought them because one of the pack females told her that she wouldn't last for seven days without using some kind of pleasure toy to help take the edge off the need that would be coursing through her. She was now very grateful that she'd taken that advice.

Pulling a purple vibrator from the box, she climbed up on the bed and rolled to her back, spreading her legs apart. The vibrator turned on with a button on the bottom and had three speeds. Her pussy was soaking wet and her clit was throbbing. She knew it wouldn't take much to set her off.

Closing her eyes, she clicked the vibrator on its lowest setting and set the humming silicone toy against her clit. Her body clenched and she gasped as she arched up, rubbing against the toy as pleasure swarmed her. With one hand she kept the vibrator on her clit and with the other she rubbed her fingers across her hard nipples.

It took only one image of Luke in her mind for her body to split apart with climax and she screamed his name, imagining that it was his tongue on her clit and not a toy, his fingers plucking and tugging at her nipples while she writhed. Plunging the vibrator into her pussy, she arched high off the bed with a sharp cry as pleasure stole her breath and her body heated and pulsed as she came again.

The bed rocked as she went limp, the vibrator slipping from her pussy and tickling her thigh. Breathing hard, she closed her eyes. She'd never come twice in a row in her life. She hadn't taken many lovers, but none of them had ever rocked her world like that vibrator.

She gazed up at the rough-hewn ceiling of the cabin and chuckled. No wonder some men didn't like sex toys. They couldn't hope to keep up. Her thoughts drifted immediately to Luke. He didn't strike her as the sort of man that would be intimidated by a sex toy, but would rather do anything to be sure that the woman he was with was satisfied. A snarl came from her throat that surprised her. She'd never really thought about the females that Luke had been with before. She knew he'd dated, the same as she had, but they'd never really talked about those people.

She reached for the vibrator and turned it off, dropping it next to her on the bed and closing her eyes. It didn't matter if Luke had been with anyone else before her, the same way that it didn't matter who came before him in her bed. From the moment that they chose to become mates, there would never be anyone else for either of them.

When the pleasure from her two orgasms subsided, she had expected that there would be a lull before her body would start to heat up again. But within minutes, her heart started to pound and her stomach started to quiver. The orgasms, although wonderful, had felt empty in some way, and she knew that it was because she was alone. She might be able to deal with the heat by artificial means, but her body knew that there was no male with her, and that left her feeling unsatisfied.

It's going to be a long week.

By the time the sun set, Eveny had come so many times that her body felt hollow from the inside out. She was physically exhausted but she was also hyper, unable to do more than doze off between sessions. She had burned out the batteries in the vibrator after the first couple hours and had trouble replacing them because her hands shook so badly. Then she'd switched to a different vibrator, a Rabbit that twisted and turned inside her pussy. Then she'd tried a bullet vibrator. They all made her come. Made her tingle with pleasure. But after the first few climaxes, she stopped feeling satisfied at all. If anything, the climaxes seemed to make her need even greater.

She contemplated getting into her car, driving to Luke, and begging him to help her, but she knew that was a pipe dream. She'd never make it the thirty miles to town. Not only because she couldn't seem to go ten minutes without trying to make herself come, but also because once she hit town, even in her car, the scent of her heat would attract the unmated males in her pack and she'd end up leading them right to Luke. They would see him as a threat and they'd kill him.

She soaked in the tub, but the hot water made her sweat and as it cooled, it chilled her until she shook. Drying off as best she could, she glanced at the kitchen and the thawed steak on the counter and knew she should cook it and try to eat, but she couldn't bring herself to stand at the stove.

She stood in the center of the cabin and looked at the bed with the crumpled sheet and box of sex toys on the floor in front of it. Then she looked at the walls of the cabin. Her wolf whined pitifully in her mind and she mentally stuck her fingers in her ears. She could see now what a bad choice she'd made in trying to go through this on her own. If she had been smart, she would have told Luke a week ago and brought condoms. Then she would have had his help with the heat but not tied him down with the mating and a baby until they'd had a chance to talk.

She wanted to smack herself for not considering that. She'd made her plan - to delay until after this heat and then give Luke plenty of time to understand the consequences of their mating - and she hadn't allowed herself to see any other alternatives.

Her stomach cramped again, and the need to have sex filled her mind. She'd definitely made a mistake. Several of them.

Lights hit the back wall of the cabin and then disappeared. She heard a vehicle pull to the side of the cabin and stop abruptly, the brakes squealing some.

Her head cocked to the side as she realized she recognized the sound of the engine. It was Luke's truck.

She moved to the bed and pulled the sheet off, wrapping it around her body. She began to walk to the door, but Luke's voice carried through it.

"Ev? Lock the front door and don't let anyone in but me."

"Luke?" she questioned, pausing with her hand on the door. Her voice was scratchy and her throat was raw from overuse. And the sound of Luke's voice made her belly clench. After all the orgasms over the course of the day, her body lit right up for him.

"Did you hear me, Ev? I fucking mean it. Don't open this door for anyone but me." He was angry. Really angry.

She swallowed hard as she heard another vehicle arrive. This engine was louder than Luke's, and she didn't know who was driving, but Luke was agitated enough that whoever it was couldn't be good.

She looked at the deadbolt that her father had installed when she was fourteen after a group of teens from another town had jimmied the door lock and gotten in and partied, trashing the place.

"It's locked, Luke."

"Baby, if things get bad, go out the back and get in your car and get the hell away from here. Got it?"

"Luke?" she asked, confused and scared.

"Baby?" he reiterated.

"I promise."

She clutched the sheet tighter to herself, went to the window next to the front door, hooked her finger in the curtain and pulled it open enough to peer out. She gasped in shock.

Luke stood on the front porch, facing the front yard and an SUV. All four doors of the SUV opened and Vince, Rufus, Barry, and Taylor climbed out. What the hell were Vince and his cronies doing here? How had they known where she was?

"What are you doing here, human?" Vince demanded.

"Protecting Eveny." Luke widened his stance and slipped his hands behind his back. She couldn't see what he was reaching for in the darkness, but her gaze traveled down his legs and she saw a baseball bat and what looked like two police batons at his feet. He was going to fight them?

Her heart began to race. Fear and relief twined together inside her. Relief that he had come for her, but fear at what he was facing.

Vince snorted and the other guys laughed. "You're only delaying the inevitable. I have *permission*."

Luke's voice came out on a snarl. "Fuck that. Acksel did not give you permission to invite your asshole friends up here to join in."

Vince laughed loudly. "Fuck Acksel."

"He's your alpha."

Vince snorted. "When he finds out what I've done, he'll be so torn up with grief that he'll go berserk, and we'll be waiting for him. He'll be crippled so badly by losing his only sister that he'll be easy pickings."

Eveny's mouth fell open. Was Vince saying he was going to rape and then kill her so that he could take over as pack alpha?

"If you want to be alpha, be a fucking man and go challenge him. Only a pussy attacks a female when she's most vulnerable." Luke said.

"You know nothing about us, human. Leave now while you can." Vince ordered.

"*You* leave now. I'm not going to tell you again."

She saw Luke pull two small canisters from his back pockets and make some motions with his thumbs.

"You ready to die, human?" Rufus growled, cracking his neck.

"For her? Absolutely."

The four males were a few dozen feet away from the porch. She didn't know what they were doing at the cabin, but she could tell from the looks on their faces, illuminated by the SUV's headlights, that they didn't have anything good planned. She didn't understand how they'd come to find out where she was, but it seemed as if Acksel was involved somehow.

Luke's hands whipped out from his back and liquid arced and splashed on the faces of Barry and Taylor, who had moved slightly closer. They howled and went down, rubbing their faces and rolling on the ground. He'd maced them. She'd never seen mace work on wolves before, so it must have been a special kind.

While the two men were growling in frustration and temporarily blinded, Luke grabbed the two batons and she heard the hiss of electricity.

Vince shouted, "Get him, Rufus."

Luke swung the batons, nailing Rufus in the head as he raced forward. Rufus snarled and righted himself quickly, snagging one of the batons with his hand. He jerked on the baton and Luke stumbled down the steps to the ground, rolling onto his back. Her heart leapt into her throat and tears stung her eyes.

Rufus lifted the baton and swung it in a downward motion, attempting to stab Luke with it, but Luke lifted the other baton and thrust it between Rufus's legs. There was a buzzing sound, and Eveny could see small flashes of electricity. Rufus froze with a strained grunting sound and then hit the ground. Luke rose to his feet, jamming the baton further against Rufus's crotch as Rufus grunted and his body jerked.

"Eight million volts, asshole," Luke said, dropping the baton and rising to his feet.

The two wolves that he'd maced were still blinded, rubbing at their eyes and trying unsuccessfully to get to their feet. "That just leaves you, Vince. Be smart and take off. She's mine."

He'd said she was his! Even in the middle of the fight, she smiled. He might not understand what she was going through right now, but he was protecting her. And doing a good job of it. Hope sprang inside her that Luke would make it through the fight and she could be with him. Now that he was here, she wanted him even more. He'd come to fight for her and was willing to go up against four of her brother's best fighters to do so.

Vince growled and Eveny saw his fangs elongate. "Acksel will never allow her to mate with a human. He would kill her first."

Eveny's breath caught in her throat at the statement and then she shook her head. Acksel would be pissed off, but he wouldn't kill her or Luke, he'd just shun them.

"He can try," Luke said.

Vince roared in fury and launched himself at Luke. Eveny gasped, her hand tightening on the curtain as she watched Vince and Luke grapple. If Vince shifted, he would tear Luke apart.

Terror swamped her. She could see Vince's eyes shining in the headlights from the SUV and knew that he was going to shift. She yelled for Luke and he shoved away from Vince and raced for the porch, grabbing the other baton with one hand and picking up the baseball bat with the other. He spun and swung out with both hands, but Vince was right behind him and knocked the baton and bat out of Luke's hands.

Luke punched Vince in the face; and Vince stumbled back and then threw himself forward and caught Luke in the stomach with his shoulder. They went to the ground together and Vince straddled Luke and began to punch him. She saw Luke get hit once. Twice. Three times. Then Luke kicked his legs and managed to pin Vince. He put his hands around Vince's throat and pressed his knee into his stomach, leaning forward with all his weight.

She saw the claws sprout from Vince's fingertips and Luke cursed loudly as Vince raked his claws down Luke's arms. But Luke didn't let go. When Vince dug his clawed hands into Luke's sides, he bellowed in pain but kept squeezing. Eveny moved to open the door but Luke seemed to sense what she was about to do.

"Eveny." He said her name loudly with an even tone that told her if she stepped outside that he would be furious.

She was as helpless as a human right now, and even though it warred with every protective instinct in her body to stay inside while Luke fought for her, she listened to him. The heat-cycle prevented her from shifting, which was her only hope in a fight against a male. She wouldn't do anything but get in the way or distract Luke. Rufus was still unconscious from the electricity. The two other wolves had crawled towards the SUV. She didn't know if they were trying to escape or looking for something to help with their blindness from the mace, but as long as they kept out of the main fight, then she didn't care what they did.

Vince tossed Luke off himself and Luke rolled on the ground and came up into a fighting stance. He was bleeding down his arms and from his sides. She could see the wetness staining his dark shirt.

Vince howled and shifted, his clothes ripping away in the process as his human form twisted and broke until a large gray wolf stood before Luke. Vince had shifted into his form during a fight, which told Eveny that Luke was beating him and Vince was going to cheat. It was unfair for a wolf to fight a human.

She pressed her palms against the window as tears filled her eyes. What hope did Luke have?

The wolf charged, and at the last minute, Luke leapt to the side and Vince passed by him, his claws digging into the dirt as he tried to round on Luke but missed. Vince snarled and bolted towards Luke, leaping into the air and landing on top of him, knocking him to the ground. There was a cracking sound and Eveny feared it was Luke's neck, but then she saw a brilliant red light and heard a wolf's pain-filled howl.

Her eyes widened as Vince's fur caught fire as Luke pressed whatever the red glow was against Vince's body. Luke shoved him away and the wolf rolled to the side, a flare sticking out of his side. The flames died quickly and Luke stood slowly and turned towards the SUV.

"Get out of here and take your friends with you," Luke said, his voice filled with fury. She'd never heard him sound so commanding.

Taylor, who had been hiding inside the SUV, came out slowly, his head ducked down in deference and his hands at his sides. He didn't speak, but moved swiftly to Vince's body and lifted him, carrying him to the SUV. Barry roused Rufus and helped him to stand. She didn't know if they could see with the mace in their eyes well enough to get back to town, and she actually didn't care.

When the SUV pulled away, she slipped to the floor in relief and let the tears fall. She'd been too keyed up to actually cry, and she shook with residual fear. Luke could have died. The last words that she would have spoken to him would have been, "I promise." Not *I love you* or *I want you to be mine.*

"Baby?" Luke knocked on the door. "They're gone. Let me in."

Her whole world centered on the sound of his voice and her wolf howled in her mind. Luke had rescued her. Saved her life. And he was here now and, yeah, she was still in heat. Her body flooded with heat immediately, all fear washed away as a tide of powerful need rolled through her.

This wasn't her plan. Her plan had been blown sky high when those wolves showed up. She was relieved that Luke had saved her, but she wasn't ready to talk to him about her heat-cycle.

What would happen if she opened the door?

What would happen if she didn't?

CHAPTER SIX

Luke watched the SUV pull away. The tires spun on the dry ground and rocks spit behind them as it lurched forward in their attempt to flee. He'd never seen wolves act so frightened before, but they sure did seem to be scared of him. Which was a good thing. He didn't want them to regroup and come back up here with reinforcements.

The smell of burnt fur and skin hung in the air and he looked at the place where Vince had been. He wasn't sure if the wolf was alive or dead, and he didn't care. He had successfully defended Eveny and even managed to live to tell the tale.

He looked down at himself. He couldn't see much in the darkness, but the spill of light from the cabin window was enough to illuminate the blood on his arms. They hurt like a bitch, as well as his sides, and some other places on his body he was sure had cuts and bruises. He didn't want Eveny to see him beat all to hell, but he needed to get into the house and make sure she was okay and then clean up. He hoped there was a medical kit in the cabin. It hadn't occurred to him to bring one. Probably because the pessimistic part of his brain didn't really think he'd survive against four wolves.

He picked up the weapons and put them back in the bag. One stun baton was dead and needed to be recharged, but the other was almost full. The mace cans were empty, but he still had two flares and the baseball bat. He didn't expect any wolves to come back tonight, but if they did then he would be prepared for them. Knocking on the cabin door, he told Eveny that the males were

47

gone and she could open the door. He could hear her crying but she didn't answer him.

He knocked again. Called her name.

When she got quiet, he knew that something was wrong.

"Baby? I'm bleeding all over the front porch. Let me in so I can clean up." He figured appealing to her desire to take care of him would work. And it did.

The door cracked open. She looked exhausted. She licked her lips. "Just to clean up?"

Frowning, he said, "What's wrong, Ev?"

"You, uh, you can't come in, Luke. Not to stay with me." She opened the door and stepped away. "The bathroom is back there, but then you have to go."

She was trembling from head to toe. Her eyes were bright gold, like coins, and her skin was flushed and dewy with sweat. He took a step towards her and her voice came out guttural and animalistic. "Don't, Luke. Please." She moved until a ratty couch was between them and clutched at the sheet that was draped around her.

He couldn't very well deal with her while he was bleeding, so he decided to clean up first and then he'd get her to talk.

"You happen to have a medical kit?"

"Under the sink."

"Don't even think about leaving, Ev. I'll be back to talk in a few minutes."

When he flicked on the bathroom light, a bare, yellowed bulb illuminated the small room. He grimaced at his reflection in the mirror. Although she had let him in, he was surprised that she hadn't tried to help him. It made him wonder what the heat-cycle was doing to her.

The medical kit under the sink was in a large fabric tote filled with much more than he expected. He knew that wolves didn't really use doctors or hospitals, and they healed quickly, but that didn't mean they didn't get injured.

He turned on the shower and stripped, getting under the tepid water to rinse off the blood and clean his wounds. He had no idea if wolf claws were dirty or not, but he decided to err on the side of caution and used an anti-bacterial wash from the kit to clean the marks. Vince had raked his claws down both of Luke's arms and gouged his sides as well, so Luke knew he would wind up with scars. But he'd wear the scars with pride because they meant that he was strong enough to protect Eveny.

When he was free of blood, he turned off the shower and got out, patting his skin dry and then securing the towel around his waist. He put Neosporin on the claw marks on his arms and laid thick gauze pads on them, securing them with tape. Then, to protect the bandages, he wrapped them in wide, self-sticking gauze. Both arms were now covered with flesh-colored bandages from bicep to wrist.

He tended the wounds on his sides in the same manner, but just taped them well instead of wrapping bandages all around his midsection. He finished by placing a small bandage over a cut on one eye and swallowing four aspirin. Tomorrow he'd be sore as hell, but tonight he was going to ignore the aches and pains and take care of his woman.

He'd never been so nervous in all his life as when he opened the bathroom door and stepped out into the cabin's main room. Eveny stood where he'd left her, using the couch to put a physical barrier between them.

Her eyes landed on his arms immediately and he could see the shine of tears in their golden depths.

"I'm going to be okay, Ev," he said in a low voice as he walked slowly towards her. He bypassed her and went to the front door and threw the lock. The sliding bolt echoed in the room in a final way. He was staying.

"You have to leave, Luke." Her voice was still low and growly, and he liked it.

He turned from the front door and faced her. "No."

Her knuckles turned white as she gripped the sheet she held against her body. A body he'd wanted to touch for years.

"Luke, it's not safe."

He cracked his neck as anger wove through him. Hadn't he just proven that he could take care of her? "Really? Because those assholes came here to rape you, Ev. Males from your own pack. From where I'm standing, it seems as if you're safer with me than alone."

Her eyes widened and she shook her head. "No, it's not safe for you to be here with *me.*"

Before he could tell her that he would be able to handle whatever her heat-cycle threw at him, she made a pained sound and doubled over, clutching her stomach.

Tired of the couch between them, Luke stormed over to her and picked her up in his arms.

She struggled weakly at first as he strode to the bed, but then she seemed to melt into him, pressing her face against his neck. He felt the gentle scrape of her teeth against his flesh and he shuddered. Laying her down on the bed, he sat next to her and put one of his hands on hers as they continued to clutch the sheet to her body.

She tensed and gritted her teeth together. Squeezing her eyes tightly shut, she said, "Please, Luke."

"Please, what? Leave you in pain? Unprotected? Your father is an idiot for thinking you'd be safe. And don't get me started on your brother."

She went still and opened her eyes slowly. "What about Acksel?"

Luke shook his head. "He's the one who told Vince where you were. Vince called his buddies to join him, but Acksel caused the problem. This might have been a safehouse, but Acksel compromised it. Their best intentions involved you getting gang-raped, and judging from their chatter about Acksel's grief, I don't think they intended to let you live. I'll deal with him after your heat. Right now, you're going to drop that death grip on the sheet and let me take care of you."

"Luke." She licked her lips and he wondered if she was thirsty. Before she could say anything else, he went to the refrigerator and opened it, looking for something cold to drink. There wasn't anything inside. He settled for filling a glass with water from the sink, and then wet a clean dish towel.

Joining her on the bed, he put the towel in his lap, hooked his hand behind her neck and lifted her gently so she could drink. She gulped the water until the cup was empty and then he settled her back on the bed. Pressing the towel lightly against her skin, he tried his best to cool her down.

She exhaled softly when he pressed the towel to her neck. "Thank you."

"I will always take care of you, Ev."

Her eyes drifted to his. "No, I mean thank you for coming for me and protecting me."

"I will always do that, too."

He tried to untangle her fingers from the sheet, but she tensed. "You still need to go, Luke."

"Not going to happen."

"You don't understand what this means. You have to go so I can do this on my own."

"I'm not going anywhere. I want you, Ev. I want to take care of you. Not just for your heat, but forever." He felt as if he were standing on the edge of a mountain, unsure whether his next step would be safe or send him plummeting to his death. "I've proven I can protect you. I can help you with this, too. I love being your friend, but I want every part of you. Forever."

He tossed the wet towel aside and rested his fingers on the edge of the towel around his waist. His cock had gone shamelessly hard the moment that she was safe. Her eyes trailed down his chest and landed where his fingers played across the material.

"No," she hissed, her eyes darkening.

"Tell me why."

"Because I might scratch you."

He shrugged and looked at his bandaged arms. Scars from her? Not a problem. "I'll live."

"I might bite you."

"I like your fangs." It was true. The first time he'd ever seen her get upset and her fangs came out, he thought they were cool. And sexy.

She sat up slowly and released the sheet. It pooled at her waist, revealing her large, firm breasts which were tipped with tight, hard nipples.

"If you make love to me, Luke," she whispered, "I'm going to let you come inside me. If that happens, then I *might* become pregnant. But you will *definitely* become my mate."

Clarity washed through him. He reached for her hands and she grasped his. "If it were easy to mate with a human then we would have done this earlier, right?"

She nodded.

"You'll lose your pack if you mate with me, because I'm human."

She blinked and tears slipped over her cheeks. "Everything. I'll lose everything. The pack will shun me and Acksel will be forced to mark me so that no other pack will want me. And my dad will have to turn his back on me and pretend that I'm dead even though I'm not. We'll have to leave town. You can't buy the bar because Acksel will forbid the pack from going there and there's not enough human business to keep it afloat. You won't be able to see your grandma unless she comes to visit us. My dad will never know his grandkids-" her voice choked off and he hugged her tightly in spite of the ache in his arms.

He didn't want her to lose her family. "I'm a selfish prick," he said, sighing as he pressed his face into her neck. "I didn't know what mating with me would mean to you or your family. I'll help you with your heat and not come inside you, and then I'll walk away so you don't have to choose between me and your family."

It might kill him, but he wanted her to be happy, and he knew she'd be happiest with her family.

She reared back like he had struck her. "No!"

Now he was confused.

"No, what?"

She shook her head almost violently. "I want you to be my mate. There isn't anyone else that I want in the world besides you. My wolf wants you. She won't accept any other males."

His heart rejoiced to hear that she wanted him to be her mate. But mating with him came at a terrible cost to her. "But your family? Your pack?"

"It'll be painful, but I can't spend the rest of my life being miserable because of a stupid wolf law that says we can't mate outside of our own kind. My dad will be sad but he'll understand. He'll want me to be happy, even if I have to leave. And he and I will figure out a way to stay in touch, I just know it." She took a deep breath. "I just wanted time to talk to you about everything."

He brushed her hair away from her face as he thought about what she was saying. "You wanted to go through the heat alone so we could talk things out for the next year? And then what?"

He was mildly amused by her plan. That was *so* Eveny. She liked to have all her ducks in a row before she did anything. That she would want to have time to prepare him for the consequences of their mating told him how much she cared for him.

"Then we'd be ready."

"I love you, Ev. I've loved you since we were kids. If you want my help, I swear on my life that I won't come inside you. When you're through the cycle, we can talk." He leaned forward and kissed her forehead. "I don't need the year to think, sweetheart. I know I can't shift. I know I'm only human. But if you'll have me, I'll be the best mate to you. I'll never regret anything that happened to see you be mine forever."

Her voice trembled as she stared at him. "You want to be mine?"

"I've always been yours, Ev."

"There isn't any going back, Luke," she said, sliding her legs around and going up on her knees. She shoved the sheet away and knelt before him, completely naked. She was so aroused that he could smell the sweet scent of her and it made his mouth water.

"I don't want to go back. I never want to go back to when I couldn't have you. After I touch you, baby, there's nothing on earth that could keep me away. Be mine."

"Yes," she hissed, leaning forward and pressing her mouth to his. Her lips hovered above his as she whispered, "Make love to me. Come inside me."

He growled. "Deep inside."

Her hands fisted in his hair and she leaned back enough to look into his eyes. "I've never let anyone come inside me, Luke. I want you to be my first. My only."

"Your mate."

CHAPTER SEVEN

Luke crushed his lips to Eveny's and pulled her into his arms, holding her tightly against him. She'd seen him shirtless before, but she'd never really touched him. Part of her wanted to take the time to explore the smooth muscles of his arms and chest and familiarize herself with every inch of his body. But the bigger part of her – the panting, howling wolf in heat – refused to waste time.

The first electric touch of their tongues sent shockwaves down her spine. He tasted wild and sweet. Their past kisses had never been like this. Needy. Hot.

Keeping her lips locked to his, she straddled his waist and reached a hand between them to tug the towel away. His erection had tented the towel, and the moment she felt the hot, hard length of him, she could think of nothing else but impaling herself on him.

Luke pulled away from her hungry mouth and gripped her wrist, pushing her hand away. "Not yet."

She strained against his grip. "Please," she pleaded, looking into his eyes.

"Not. Yet."

He pushed her backwards until her back pressed against the mattress. She hissed out a breath as her sensitized skin pressed into the fitted sheet. It had felt so good to be against Luke's body. It hadn't made her skin ache. But the sheet – which she knew was actually quite soft – felt like razor blades.

Luke leaned over her and stroked his fingers down the center of her chest. Her breath hitched in her throat.

"I've wanted to touch you for so long, Ev," he said in a husky tone. His fingers circled around her lower stomach and then trailed upwards until he ran them along the underside of one breast. He cupped her breast with his hand and rubbed his thumb around her nipple. The nipple was already hard and straining, but it tightened further the longer he touched it.

She whimpered and gripped his biceps. His lips brushed hers.

"I want to take hours with you, baby, but I know you're hurting. There's just one thing I need to do first."

She hadn't realized she'd closed her eyes until they flew open when he bent over and sucked her nipple into his mouth. The wet heat of his mouth overwhelmed her, making her stomach contract and her body arch up. The hand that cupped her breast slid down her body and pushed her legs apart. She buried her fingers in his hair and held him to her breast as he sucked and teased her nipple and stroked his fingers along her sex. She'd never seen anything as erotic as Luke sucking on her breast, with his cheeks hollowing and a look of rapture on his face.

"Luke!" she shouted as he plunged two fingers inside her pussy. Her hands fisted in his hair as her hips lifted.

Before he had come to save her, she had been physically and mentally exhausted. Her orgasms had taken longer and longer to achieve by herself, and the thrum of the vibrator had started to set her teeth on edge. But just one touch from Luke and she was standing on the threshold of pleasure once more; better pleasure than she'd thought possible.

She thought he would be tender, but he seemed to sense that she didn't want tender right now. Tender could come later, when the heat was over and her body wasn't screaming for his cock. His fingers pounded into her and she tugged him from her breast with her fists in his hair until she could kiss him. She whimpered and moaned into his mouth as his fingers worked inside her.

Pleasure raced over her body like electricity and she cried out, her hands clutching his shoulders and her nails digging into his flesh. He kept the orgasm flowing by thumbing her clit until he had wrenched from her every ounce of pleasure that he could.

He kneed her legs apart. Lifting his hand slowly so she could see how wet his fingers were, she watched as he licked his fingers, closing his eyes as if he had just tasted something exquisite.

The heat-cycle began to rise in her again. Her climax had just eased the need, but hadn't erased it completely.

He planted his hand next to her head on the bed and fisted his cock, guiding it to the entrance of her body. His eyes held hers, the blue depths darkening as he pushed inside her still-clenching pussy and went into a push-up over her. His hips thrust forward until he was buried to the hilt.

She gasped as he filled her completely, their bodies perfectly, tightly wed together. Nothing had ever felt as good as her mate filling her and she groaned mindlessly and arched harder against him, his name a breathless chant on her lips.

Her hands slipped from his shoulders down to his sides, just above the bandages, and she wrapped her legs around his waist.

"I love you, Eveny." He kissed her, pressing his hips tighter to her.

Her hands squeezed his sides as her thighs hugged him. "I love you, too, Luke."

He stroked out of her slowly and she felt every inch of him until just the thick head remained inside. He paused for just a second and then he thrust forward, filling her completely. She slipped her arms around him further, one hand resting high on his back and the other lower, just above his ass. She knew she was scratching him, but she couldn't seem to stop marking him over and over.

He began to thrust harder and faster, leaning forward and gripping the headboard for leverage with one strong arm. She met his thrusts, feeling pleasure bloom inside her once more as he pushed her to orgasm. He gazed down at her as he fucked her hard, pushing the breath from her lungs with each thrust, his body glistening with sweat and his muscles straining.

Her brain began to fog over as her orgasm grew, twisting and coiling inside her until she thought she would burn from the inside out. Her body locked down on his as her climax crested, and she screamed. She felt her claws spring from her fingertips and dig into his flesh and her fangs erupt from her gums. She snarled and leaned up to sink her fangs into his neck and mark him as hers forever.

All she could focus on was the feel of Luke's flesh between her teeth and the metallic taste of his blood on her tongue. His hard and fast rhythm faltered and she felt his cock thicken just a moment before he groaned her name and came. The rush of his hot come inside her calmed her raging libido, and she felt utterly relaxed.

Releasing his flesh, she licked across the marks and then hugged her arms around him as he exhaled and lowered his body to hers. He kept most of his weight off of her, but she still felt the heaviness of him, and the delicious feeling of his cock still buried deeply.

This was what had been missing from her life all those years. The intimate connection between herself and her mate. Luke wasn't just her mate. He was her heart. And the only man that had ever held her heart in his hands.

He kissed her neck and then rolled to his side, carrying her with him. "I've had a lot of fantasies about you over the years, sweetheart, but that was a thousand times better than anything my brain has ever come up with."

She chuckled and rested her head on his shoulder. "You've been part of my fantasies for a long time, too."

"Oh? Anything particularly naughty that we can do after your heat is over?"

She tipped her face up to look at him. His eyes were bright and his lips were curled up in amusement. "I've always wanted to try something sweet and sticky, like whipped cream or chocolate syrup."

His fingers played across her back and he chuckled. "Sounds like you could become my favorite dessert."

She could faintly feel the heat-cycle ramping up again, and while she still had her wits about her, she asked him to tell her what brought him – and the other wolves – up to the cabin.

As he told her about overhearing Acksel and then Vince, she knew that she was staring at him in utter disbelief.

His brows furrowed. "You believe me, don't you?"

"Of course. I know you wouldn't lie to me. Although I talked to some of the females about going through the heat on my own, I never said I was leaving town. The only people – besides you – who knew where I was were Acksel and my dad. There's no way my dad would have told any of the males that showed up here where I was. That leaves Acksel."

He was very quiet and she straightened her arms and looked down at him. "What?"

He frowned. "You don't want to know what I'm thinking about right now."

"Let's not start with secrets, Luke, please."

He exhaled and stroked her cheeks with his thumbs. "I want to kill Acksel, baby. I want to fucking break his neck and kill the assholes that came up here thinking they would rape you."

She stared into his determined blue eyes, taking in the snarl on his lips and the intense anger that radiated from the sapphire depths. He was one of the most even-tempered men she'd ever known. But the man underneath her was all alpha male. She felt incredibly blessed to have him as her mate. "Luke?"

"Yeah, baby?"

"I love you."

His brow arched and the snarl faded to a tender smile. "Even after all I just said?"

"You proved you could protect me, Luke." She gently touched the fang marks on his throat. "I marked you as my mate. Your come is inside me. We're together for the long haul."

His smile broadened. "Better or worse?"

Nodding, she leaned down and kissed him. He groaned as he opened his mouth to her questing tongue and the need that had slowly been building within her rose to a fever pitch.

He rolled them, not breaking the kiss, and slipped two fingers inside her pussy. Within seconds she was screaming her pleasure and writhing under his talented fingers. As he pushed his hard cock inside her, she threw her arms around his neck and kissed him, and they made love again.

Nothing had ever felt as perfect as what she experienced with her best friend and mate. Regardless of what waited for them after the heat was over, she knew that taking Luke as her mate was worth it all. It hadn't really even been a choice. He was the *only* one for her. The only male that would ever be her mate.

CHAPTER EIGHT

Luke rolled to his back and stretched, stifling a groan as his muscles burned and ached. He'd made love to Ev four times overnight and given her several orgasms with his fingers and tongue in between rounds while his body recovered.

He'd never had sex so many times in one night, and he'd worried that he wouldn't be enough for her, but after the fourth time, when her body seemed to calm down as it did for a while after each round, she fell asleep in his arms and didn't rouse right away.

He'd enjoyed holding her and watching her sleep, but he didn't waste time staying awake. He wanted to rest as much as possible before her heat started up again.

His eyes popped open as he realized that he was in bed alone. Sitting up, he found her standing at the front window, the sheet wrapped around her body. She looked peaceful as she stared out into the woods surrounding the cabin.

He slipped out of bed and joined her, putting his arms around her and resting his chin on top of her head. "How are your wounds?" she asked, her fingers touching the edges of the bandages on his arms.

"Healing. Are you okay, baby?"

"I feel great, actually." Her voice had a little bit of awe to it.

"You do?"

She turned in his arms and smiled up at him. "The heat's over."

For a moment he wasn't sure he'd heard her right. "What?"

"It's over," she repeated.

"But it was supposed to last for a week, right?"

She seemed highly amused by his inability to understand what was going on. And then he understood.

Holy crap, she was pregnant.

She reached for him, concern on her face. "Are you okay? You said you understood what might happen if we had sex without protection."

He snorted and swept her up in his arms. "I think I remember health class, baby." He dropped her to the bed and settled next to her, peeling the sheet away from her beautiful body and resting his palm on her stomach. "Sorry I'm a little slow this morning. There was this incredible she-wolf in bed with me last night and she kept begging for my cock."

"Sounds like a real trial," she laughed.

"Oh yeah, I'm exhausted." He chuckled and kissed her. "Tell me about the baby we made, Ev." He'd never said something that filled him with such joy. His best friend – his mate – was carrying his child.

He didn't think he'd ever seen her smile so brightly. Her hand rested on top of his. "I think it's why I was able to go sleep after the last time we made love. I was told that when the male's seed plants, the heat stops immediately, but I was too tired last night to figure out why I was able to actually fall asleep without the heat getting so bad again."

"Human women don't realize they're pregnant until after they miss their periods. Wolves are really amazing."

"My people are pretty different biologically. I don't actually have a period. My body is only ready for pregnancy during the heat, so I can't get pregnant any other time during the year and I don't need regular birth control."

He mulled that over for a minute. "So next fall, if we don't want to have a baby, then I should use condoms?"

"It depends. If I'm still nursing our baby, then I won't go through the heat-cycle next fall. Once the baby weans, then I'll go through the next heat-cycle after that for sure. We can decide whether we want to have another baby when the time comes, and if not, then yes you'd need to use condoms."

She lifted her hand to cup his cheek. "You're going to be a great father, Luke. I know it."

Pride swelled in his chest. "You're going to be a great mom, too, Ev."

He slipped his hand down her stomach and cupped her sex. She moaned softly, her teeth digging into her bottom lip. He realized that she did that whenever she was turned on.

He nuzzled her neck and nipped at her pulse. She spread her legs, lifting her hips in invitation, and he smiled. He'd wondered last night if she was reacting so strongly to him because of the heat-cycle, but as he pushed a finger inside her and felt her hot wetness, he knew that her reaction to him wasn't fueled by anything but her feelings towards him.

He pulled his finger away and pinched her clit lightly between his finger and thumb and she moaned, one hand fisting in the sheet and the other clutching his arm. Tugging lightly, he rubbed the swollen bud and watched her body begin to tremble.

He released her clit and she whimpered as he leaned over and kissed her. "I want you to come around my cock, baby." He rolled off the bed and found the box of sex toys that had gotten shoved under the bed. When he noticed them after the first time they made love, she had kicked the box under the bed and said she didn't need them any longer because his cock was better than any battery-operated toy. He'd been curious as to whether she'd thought about him while she was playing, and she'd blushed but assured him that she had.

There were several different vibrators shaped like cocks, but since he wasn't trying to replace his cock but instead give her some extra pleasure, he chose a small egg-shaped vibrator that had a thin cord attached to a remote. The remote said it was called a Bullet Vibe, and he lifted it from the box and clicked the button to turn it on low. As it hummed to life in his palm, Eveny sat up in surprise and looked at him.

After testing out the other two speeds, he wiggled his brows at her and said, "On your hands and knees, baby."

She looked at him silently for a moment and then rolled fluidly to her knees, spreading her legs apart. He turned off the vibrator and climbed behind her. Placing his hand on her neck, he pushed gently and she lowered her head to the mattress and spread her legs apart further. He stroked her soaked pussy with his finger and she trembled.

He moved between her spread legs and slid his cock into her hot body. The tight heat of her was almost his undoing, but he seated himself fully inside her and then took a deep breath, grabbing hold of his control so he didn't come right away.

Switching on the bullet, he turned it on high and reached around her with one hand. Palming the vibrating toy, he rested his hand against her pussy and pressed the vibrator against her clit. She reared up with a sharp cry of pleasure; he pushed her shoulder down roughly and she fell to the mattress with a whimpering moan. He could feel the high vibrations through her body and knew he wouldn't last long. He kept the vibrator pressed to her clit and began to fuck her hard. He pistoned his cock in and out of her pussy as she groaned and writhed, her hands gripping the sheet underneath her.

Her pussy gripped him suddenly and she cried out as she came. He kept thrusting into her, ignoring the orgasm that tingled at the base of his spine and driving into her. He slid his hand up her spine and fisted his hand in her hair, jerking her body upright and pressing the vibrator more firmly against her pussy.

Her hands gripped his thighs and her nails dug into him. He bit her neck, gripping her flesh with his teeth at the juncture where her shoulder met her neck. She screamed his name again, raking her nails up his thighs and trembling. He let himself go as his climax poured over him, and he let her fall forward to the bed and followed, thrusting into her as his cock spasmed.

He kissed the place on her neck where he had bitten her. His teeth had broken through her skin and she was bleeding slightly.

"Luke?" she said weakly, shivering.

"Yeah, baby?" He kissed the mark again.

"The-the vibe?"

He chuckled and pulled his hand out from underneath her body, tugging the buzzing toy with him.

"Sorry, love."

She breathed a sigh of relief. "It's okay."

Turning off the vibrator, he leaned over and placed it on the nightstand and then settled on his side next to her. "Was I too rough?"

She turned her head so she was looking at him. Her eyes, which had been golden throughout her heat, were now back to their normal, beautiful gray. "No. I loved it."

He sighed and stroked his fingers lightly down her spine. "Is it okay that I bit you?"

She smiled. "I loved that, too. You can bite me anytime."

He grinned. "That goes doubly for you, too."

She yawned. He asked, "Want to take a nap or do you want me to make you something to eat?"

"Both? And a shower. And we need to talk."

He nodded and went to the freezer to pull out two steaks. It took longer to cook them because they were frozen solid, but he knew she was hungry and hadn't eaten since the heat had taken over. They ate in the bed and he cut up her steak and fed it to her, reveling in being able to take care of all of her needs.

While they ate, she told him what she thought would happen when they got back to Wilde Creek, and explained what Acksel would do to her. He grimaced.

"He has to, Luke," she insisted.

"I don't think anyone has a right to stick their claws into another wolf's arms just because that wolf happens to be mated to a human. It's barbaric."

She shrugged, but nodded. "If we were to just take off, Acksel would most likely come after us and then he'd want to fight you."

"I don't care about that." He'd do anything to keep her safe.

She shook her head. "It's not that I think you would fail, Luke, because I honestly don't know. But I don't want you to fight my brother because I don't think *I* could take it."

He nodded in understanding. "Should we stay here for the week or do you want to head home?"

She exhaled slowly and looked around the cabin. "It didn't seem like such a bad place to be when I was so consumed by the heat. Now, though, I kinda want to go home. Even though it means we'll probably have to pack a bag and leave tonight."

He frowned. "So soon?"

She nodded and stood, stretching. The light from the windows caught her curves and made his brain go numb. "It would be best if we went straight to my dad and told him everything. When Acksel finds out I'm back so soon, he'll figure out that my heat-cycle is over because I'm pregnant and he'll probably blow a gasket. My dad can help with that."

Luke got off the bed and stood next to her. "Do you think Acksel knows that I'm here? Vince might be dead. If he's not, then he was seriously injured.

"I don't know. I'm not sure if those guys would tell anyone that they got beaten by a human." She smiled suddenly and laughed. "Male wolves think they're so superior to humans, but you beat four of them. I'd say that you're pretty damn near perfect."

He kissed her. "What do you mean '*near* perfect'?"

She grinned so broadly that he was surprised her cheeks didn't hurt. "You hog the bed."

"Yeah?" He bent and grabbed her, tossing her over his shoulder. "You kicked me twice in your sleep."

She pinched his ass and laughed. "At least neither of us snore."

"Thank goodness for small miracles."

After showering, making love in the shower, and then showering again, they dried off and dressed. The claw marks on his arms and body were healing well, and he bandaged them again. He cleaned up while she packed up her car, and then he followed her back towards town. They went straight to her dad's house, and Luke wasn't surprised to find him in the backyard standing in front of the grill. He never used the stove in the house unless the weather was so bad he couldn't get the grill lit.

"Hi Dad," Eveny said, standing on the deck next to Luke, their hands twined together.

He looked over his shoulder in surprise. "You aren't supposed to be here for a week, honey." He eyed Luke speculatively, his eyes latching onto their hands.

Luke had a lot of respect for Dade. He had always treated Luke respectfully, not as if he were a second-class citizen the way that some wolves did.

"Sir," Luke started, but Dade held up his hands.

"It looks like there's a story to be told, so let's go inside and talk." He turned off the grill and lifted what appeared to be chicken breasts onto a platter.

Eveny cast a supportive smile at Luke and led him into the house. In the family room, Luke sat next to Eveny, and Dade sat across from them in a recliner. Luke told Dade everything, from Acksel's betrayal to Vince's invitation to his friends.

Dade was quiet for a few moments after the story was over. Then he leaned over, picked up the coffee table and threw it across the room. He howled, and the sound was pure rage.

"I'll fucking kill him!" Dade shouted.

Eveny stood up, but Luke grabbed her, shoving her behind his back for protection. "Dade!" he yelled, stepping backwards and taking Eveny with him. "Calm the fuck down."

Dade turned and snarled. "My son nearly got my daughter gang-raped and killed. And you want me to calm down?"

"I want you to not throw any more tables."

Dade bared his teeth and his fangs were elongated, but Luke wasn't worried. The anger wasn't directed at him, just at the situation. Dade spun and smashed his fist against the wall, denting it. Shaking his hand, he huffed, cracking his neck. "We need to talk to Acksel. Now."

Eveny gripped Luke's arms and peeked around him. "Dad, Acksel made a mistake."

Even Luke felt a growl well in his chest at that remark. "That's the understatement of the century, Ev."

She persisted. "Acksel was acting like an alpha, not my brother or your son. I don't know why he did it, and I hate him a little bit for what could have happened, but he's still my brother. He's still your son."

"He swore to me that he would let you go through the heat alone. He lied."

"Dad, Luke saved my life and I'm mated to him. If Acksel hadn't interfered, I would still be miserable. Acksel behaved irresponsibly and irrationally, but I got Luke because of it. He proved he was worthy to be my mate, even though I never doubted it." She paused and moved from behind Luke's back to his side. He immediately slid his arm around her shoulders and hugged her close. "Regardless of what Acksel did, the result is that I'm mated to a human and it's against our pack's traditions. You can't protect me from getting kicked out of the pack for taking Luke as my mate. You never wanted to be alpha, so you won't fight Acksel, and if you call him out in public he's going to have no choice but to put you in your place. I'm fine now. Better than fine."

"She's carrying my child, Dade. I know she's going to be shunned because of it, and I don't see any reason to stress the situation further. I wanted to kill Acksel at first, too, but he'll have to live with the knowledge that males he trusted betrayed him and it cost him his family. I know him well enough to know that he's going to go nuts when he finds out. If he doesn't already know."

"We came back so I could get out of the pack and we could be on our way to a new life."

Some of the rage leaked way from Dade's eyes. "I'm going to leave, too."

"Dad?"

He sighed. "Do you really think that I would go the rest of my life never seeing you or my grandbaby again?

Luke was surprised at Dade's statement. "You've lived in Wilde Creek your whole life."

Dade shrugged and walked over to the coffee table, which lay tilted against one wall. He righted it and ran his fingers over a crack through the center of it. "I'd rather leave here and still have you two in my life. What kind of father would I be to just watch you walk away, Eveny? I own a few acres of property around the cabin and can build another house for myself, and we can build onto the cabin for you both and turn it into a real house."

Eveny sniffled and walked to her dad, hugging him tightly. "Thanks, Dad."

Luke thought of his own father, who would have made a similar selfless decision. This was exactly the kind of father he wanted to be, too. One who would sacrifice anything for his kids.

Eveny came back to Luke's arms and Dade looked at him. "If you're wondering why I'm not surprised by you two getting together, it's because I always knew that you were meant for each other."

Eveny gasped. "You never said anything."

Dade raised a brow. "It's not my place to tell you who to be with, darlin'. You have to live with your choices and I didn't want to interfere. I decided a while ago that if you chose to mate with Luke that I would go with you, so it's not something I arrived at lightly. Acksel will still see us away from town, I'm sure of it. So I'm not really losing anything, but I am gaining a grandbaby and a son-in-law. When your heat came up, I thought you might actually choose your obligation to the pack over your heart's desire. It's why I suggested you could go through the heat alone in the cabin. I knew it would be hard on you, but you didn't seem ready to talk to Luke and I wasn't going to force you to deal with it. I'm glad you didn't choose the pack over your heart."

She looked up at Luke. "I'm glad I didn't, too."

"What now?" Luke asked.

Dade exhaled slowly and rested his hands on his hips. "I think the first thing we need to do is get you two packed up as quickly as possible. I'll stay with Eveny and make sure that she's safe and you can go pack up your place. You don't have to pack up everything right now, just enough for a few weeks." He glanced at his watch. "Don't take any longer than an hour to pack, and we'll meet up there at three-thirty."

Eveny frowned. "Shouldn't we stay together?"

Dade shook his head. "Luke's not part of the pack and no one will think anything of him being around. You're the one that will draw curiosity, which is why I'm going to stick by you and we're going to get going as fast as possible."

Luke walked Eveny to her apartment and kissed her soundly. "I'll see you at three-thirty. Call me if you get into trouble."

She leaned into him and hugged her arms around him tightly. "Don't be late."

Tipping her chin up, he brushed his lips across hers and said, "I won't be, sweetheart."

He darted down the steps, climbed into his truck and watched as Dade, carrying two suitcases, walked up the stairs to Eveny's apartment and headed inside. He knew that Dade would keep her safe. It warred with him to leave her side, but the faster he got packed, the better.

It didn't take him long to get back to his place, and he grabbed a duffel bag from the hall closet and began shoving clothes into it. When it was stuffed full, he dropped it at the front door and grabbed a backpack, which he filled with as many bathroom and kitchen items as he could find. It took longer to pack up then he thought, and before he knew it, almost an hour had passed.

Since he'd promised that he wouldn't be late, he shouldered the backpack, grabbed his keys and the duffel, and opened the door.

A fist flew at his face so fast he barely registered the sight before pain bloomed in his head and everything went dark.

CHAPTER NINE

Eveny paced on the small front porch of the cabin, chewing her thumbnail and glancing at the path where Luke's truck would appear when he arrived. Which should have happened twenty minutes earlier.

Even though she had no signal, she kept checking her cell. Her dad leaned against the door jam and folded his arms. He inclined his head to the side and she knew he was listening for Luke's truck. His brows furrowed.

She chewed on her bottom lip and clenched and unclenched her hands. "It's not like Luke to be late."

"We have no reception up here; he might have gotten held up at the bar. It could be totally innocent."

"Could be, but what if it's not?"

She turned to move off the step and her dad's grip on her arm stopped her. "We'll go together, Eveny. If there's nothing wrong, then you can ride back up here when we find him. *If* something is wrong, then it's best if we're together."

She nodded, finding it hard to speak past the lump in her throat. Within minutes, they were on their way back to town. The thirty-mile ride felt like it took hours as she kept her eyes peeled, hoping to see his truck along the way. Her dad pulled into the parking lot behind the bar, where Luke's apartment was and everything in her world narrowed down to the scene before her. Luke's truck was pulled up next to the stairs that led up to his apartment, and the door of his apartment was wide open. She leapt out of the truck and raced up the stairs. A backpack and bag were lying in the doorway;

she scented Luke's blood and found splashes of it in the small foyer and on the stairs.

She spun and looked down at her dad. His somber look made fear lodge in her chest.

"Depending on when they grabbed him, they could have had him for over an hour, darlin'."

Tears filled her eyes and she blinked quickly, not wanting to break down. Luke had stood up for her against four males. He was still alive. She knew it. She could *feel* it.

Racing down the steps, she joined her dad and said, "He's probably at Acksel's. Are you with me?"

"You know I am," he growled.

The town seemed almost empty as they drove to Acksel's home. It was eerie. When her dad turned onto Acksel's street, her heart nearly stopped at the sight of all the vehicles lining both sides of the street. The whole pack appeared to be there, and that didn't bode well for Luke.

Her dad didn't bother to find a place to park on the street; he pulled up onto Acksel's lawn in a space between two cars and parked. She jumped out and raced towards the back of the house, but her dad restrained her.

"You have to be smart, darlin'. He's being the alpha now, and it's possible that he's reacting to lies told by the males that came for you. Whatever happens, stick with the truth."

She swallowed hard and nodded. Her dad kissed her forehead, and they moved together around the side of the moderate-sized brick home towards the backyard. She could hear people speaking and occasional cheers, and as she and her dad cleared the house, the sight before her made her stomach drop into her feet.

The pack was gathered in Acksel's backyard in a wide semi-circle. In the center of the circle, Luke was chained to what had once been a metal post for a laundry line. His arms were stretched over his head and shackled to the top of the post. He was gagged and his shirt was missing. His upper body and arms were cut and bleeding, and his head was hanging down.

"This is what we do to humans who kill our males," Acksel shouted.

The pack cheered as Rufus moved from behind Acksel and punched Luke in the side. She saw Luke's body absorb the hit and heard his faint grunt of pain.

Clearing her head of her worried thoughts so she could handle things right, she strode forward into the circle and said in a loud voice, "I petition the alpha for the right to speak on behalf of the human, Luke Elrich."

The crowd quieted.

Acksel turned to her and she met his gaze. Rage filled his eyes as he snarled. His body was covered with sweat, his dark hair plastered to his forehead. His eyes were the golden color of his wolf, and his claws and fangs were elongated.

"There is no mercy here for the human who struck our male, Vince, with his truck and killed him," Acksel's voice was dark, his words sharp like blades.

"I came to tell you the truth, alpha," she clutched her hands into fists at her side, keeping her eyes on her brother.

"I have the truth!" Acksel shouted, gesturing towards Rufus, Barry, and Taylor, who were nearby.

She felt her dad step closer to her. "An alpha is wise enough to hear both sides of the story before he does something irreparable like sentence a human to death."

Acksel snarled and gnashed his teeth.

Eveny wanted to go to Luke so badly that her legs trembled, but she didn't dare. Showing any sign of affection for Luke at the moment would only make Acksel even more furious.

"Four males showed up at the cabin yesterday with the intention of taking me against my will."

Acksel's mouth dropped open.

She pointed to Luke. "That human overheard Vince invite Barry, Rufus, and Taylor to join him at the cabin where I went to endure my heat-cycle alone, and to take me against my will. Vince spoke in a way that led him to believe I would not survive what he and his friends planned to do to me, and they were planning to use your grief against you and challenge you for the alpha position. The human came to protect me, and he succeeded."

Acksel snapped his teeth together and a muscle twitched under his eye. "A human could not stand up against one wolf, let alone four."

"I watched him with my own eyes. He fought bravely and honorably, and killed Vince only after he shifted into his wolf form and attacked him. The wounds on Luke's arms aren't from running over a wolf, but from defending himself and me."

She closed the distance between herself and her brother. Looking up into his eyes, she saw the war in their gray depths. Taking his hand, she placed it on her stomach. "He's my mate, Acksel. His seed grows in my belly. I know that I have to leave the pack in shame, but I'm not ashamed of taking Luke as my mate. He protected me when it could have cost him his life. Will you take my mate from me now, Acksel? Alpha? Brother?"

She stopped fighting the tears that had threatened since she'd seen Luke's blood on the steps of his apartment. Acksel's fingers flexed on her stomach and he dropped his hand and looked at their dad.

"If you look at Luke's truck, you'll see it hasn't been damaged at all," their dad said. "You were lied to and your sister could have died."

Acksel swallowed hard and stepped back. Eveny felt like she was looking at a stranger. Would Acksel kill Luke? Would he believe her? She laid her hands on her stomach and looked at Luke. His head was lifted and he was looking at her. One eye was purple and swollen shut, but the other eye was staring right at her. She could feel how much he loved her.

Acksel spun and howled. Rufus, Barry, and Taylor backed away, but just a snap of Acksel's fingers brought his second in command, Auro, to the group and he and several other wolves stopped them from leaving.

"Take the human down," Acksel said loudly. "I find no fault with him."

The pack murmured unhappily; Acksel froze and then lifted his head and howled again. Deeper. Angrier. The sound tore through the pack and everyone fell to their knees, including her and her father, as Acksel reminded them that he was alpha.

Eveny watched as Acksel moved to the group that was holding the three men who had come with Vince, and she heard them say she was lying and that they had told him the truth. Her dad touched her shoulder and they rose together and moved to Luke.

Pack members watched her as she untied the gag and tossed it aside. "Oh, Luke, I'm so sorry," she touched his jaw with her fingertips.

His head lolled to the side and the corner of his mouth lifted in a small smile. "Love you."

Tears spilled over her cheeks. "I love you, too."

He groaned through clenched teeth as her dad loosened the chain and pulled the pins that held the shackles closed. Luke fell to his knees and she supported his upper body as much as she could, unable to see clearly through the tears.

"Are you safe?" he whispered.

"Yeah, Luke. We both are," she promised.

He sighed in relief and then went limp. She almost went down with the sudden weight, but her dad lifted him up in his arms. "Come on, darlin'."

She brushed the grass from her knees as she stood, and looked at Acksel as he gestured angrily. The three that had come to the cabin were forced to their knees. She shuddered as she and her dad left the clearing with Luke. She liked to tease Acksel about being alpha, but she knew what a hard job he had. She and her brother had grown up in this town and knew everyone, human and wolf. Acksel was facing off against men that he had known his whole life.

Maybe leaving the pack for love was the safest thing she could do. Not only for herself and Luke, but for their future kids. She didn't want their kids to be held to outdated beliefs. Punished for loving someone who was different.

She wanted better for her family, and she wasn't going to find it in Wilde Creek.

CHAPTER TEN

Acksel had never felt such fury as he stared at the three males. He had known Barry, Rufus, and Taylor his whole life. Considered them friends. And they'd tried to get him to kill Luke.

He glanced over his shoulder to where his father was carrying Luke while Eveny walked beside them. Eveny's face was pale, her eyes filled with worry. He knew that he'd crossed a line somewhere in the last hour. If another human in town had hit and killed a wolf, he would have turned them over to the local police. But he'd smelled Eveny on Luke, seen her mark on his neck, and that had enraged him. He hadn't stopped to question his pack members about the wild tale they'd spun of the human purposely hitting Vince and killing him. He had ignored the burns and singed fur that spoke of something other than getting hit by a truck. He'd wanted to have a reason to rough the human up.

Luke hadn't even really defended himself. Only once had he said that he did kill Vince, but it hadn't been with his truck. Acksel hadn't given him a chance to explain. He'd called for a pack meeting, inviting males and females to watch as he held the human accountable for Vince's death. They'd wanted blood. And he'd allowed it. Encouraged it. Turned a deaf ear to the part of him that knew it wasn't right to make a person helpless and beat them within an inch of their lives.

Dread pooled in his stomach. He'd done a lot of shitty things to become alpha, but he'd never outright abused his power. Where had his calm head gone?

"You have one opportunity to tell me the truth," Acksel said.

All three males refused to raise their heads to meet his gaze. That alone spoke volumes. Rufus finally cleared his throat. "It was as your sister said, alpha. Vince invited us to join him for her heat-cycle. He did not care whether she lived or not, and knew that you would be vulnerable in your grief whether she was hurt or dead."

He felt the betrayal like a crushing weight on his shoulders. His pack members – males he'd considered friends – were willing to attack his sister when she was at her most vulnerable. The best possible scenario was that she would have been pregnant and mated to one of them, a male that thought nothing of sharing her with his friends. The worst was that they could have killed her in a sexual frenzy. Regardless of the outcome of her life, they had planned to challenge him and use her against him as he'd always feared would happen.

But he was no better than they were. He'd broken a promise to his dad. He'd betrayed his sister.

He would deal with the males and then he would deal with his sister.

"Chain them up," he ordered and strode purposefully to the pole that was streaked with Luke's blood. The pack watched with curiosity, remaining where they were until he dismissed them.

He spoke in a loud, clear voice as the three males were chained to the pole. "I will not tolerate lies within this pack, or those that betray any pack members. These males attempted to attack a female during her most vulnerable time, and were beaten by a human. Then they attempted to frame the human for the death of one of our pack members. For these crimes, I sentence them to the same beating that they administered against the human, and then to banishment from the pack and Wilde Creek for the remainder of their days."

There were unhappy murmurings from the pack, but he growled loudly and threateningly and no one spoke up on their behalf.

He stalked forward and punched Rufus in the face. His head struck the pole and he grunted as blood welled from his nose and his upper lip split. He punched Barry and Taylor as well, and then stepped aside and directed Auro and the handful of males that had helped restrain them, to finish the job.

Blow after blow, the males begged for mercy, but Acksel tuned them out. Luke hadn't begged. Hadn't shed a tear. He wondered now if he'd been thinking of Eveny. It was true that Acksel didn't particularly like humans, but Luke had always been good to Eveny. And she clearly loved him enough to walk away from everything.

For an hour, he watched the males being struck again and again, and then he called a halt to the proceedings. The three were hanging limply from their chains, bleeding profusely. He let loose his beast enough for his eyes to change and his hands to partially shift into paws, and he lifted his voice. "I separate you from the Wilde Creek Pack from this day forward, Rufus Eddinger. For the span of your life, there is a mark upon your head. If you should step foot or paw inside this town, you will forfeit your life, according to our laws."

Acksel slashed his claws across Rufus's bicep and the male moaned pitifully and hung his head. Acksel performed the marking for the other two males and stepped away.

"Remove them and take them out of town," he spoke to Auro. "They can make arrangements for someone to pack up their things."

"Right away, alpha," Auro said and turned around and took action.

Acksel dismissed the pack, reminding them that he was alpha and what had transpired that day was dictated by their traditions. He waited until the yard was empty and then he went into the house and shut the door.

Picking up his cell from the kitchen counter, he called his father.

"I'll want to speak with you, Eveny, and Luke in five days. Until that time, I'm making no rulings on their relationship or membership within the pack."

"I understand," his dad said. "Anything you'd like me to tell your sister?"

Acksel swallowed past the lump in his throat. "Tell her I'm sorry."

CHAPTER ELEVEN

When Luke woke, his head was pounding and he couldn't see out of one eye. Every bone in his body ached, but his only thought was of Eveny.

"Hey, I'm here. Don't move," Eveny said.

"I can't see you." His voice was rough and his throat was raw.

The bed shifted and she leaned over him so he could see her. She blinked away tears. "Can you see me now?" She gave him a watery smile.

The fear that had taken root in his heart the moment he woke up eased slightly. "Yeah. You okay?"

She chuckled and wiped at a tear that slipped down her cheek. "You got beaten all to hell by my pack and you're asking me if I'm okay?" She sniffled and nodded. "I'm good and so is the baby. Can I get you anything? How are you feeling?"

"I'm okay if you're okay, Ev." And that was the truth.

She told him that he'd been unconscious for five hours and that her dad had called in the pack doctor, who'd examined him. "He bandaged your wounds, and gave you some medicine, and said he'd come back after you were awake. I got to give you a sponge bath." She laughed and he groaned.

"I missed it? Damn."

She kissed his cheek softly. "I'll give you as many as you want."

Although part of Luke wanted to fall back into unconsciousness, he knew that lying around wasn't going to be doing anyone any favors, so with some help from Eveny, he managed to sit up.

The pack doctor came by a half hour later, while Eveny was feeding him some chicken broth. After examining him, the doctor, whose name was Gedding, said, "You've got a couple of bruised ribs and a mild concussion. I won't know if there's any damage to your eyesight until the swelling goes down."

Luke asked about infection from the claw marks.

"It's unlikely you would get an infection unless you were attacked by a wolf that had been in his shift a while and had dirty claws. However, I already gave you a tetanus shot when you were unconscious, along with an anti-inflammatory and pain medication. I'll leave pills with your mate and you can take them as needed. Take it easy and give me a call in another couple of days when the swelling goes down in that eye."

"Thanks, Doc," Luke said.

Eveny and Dade thanked him, and Dade, who had brought the doctor into Eveny's apartment, walked him to the door. Turning around, he leaned against the door and said, "We've got five days before we have to meet with Acksel."

"What for?" Luke asked.

Eveny said, "He's going to banish me from the pack. He's giving you time to heal and us time to pack."

Luke had heard what happened to the three males who had told Acksel that he'd killed Vince with his truck. He thought Acksel should have chained himself up to the pole and let his pack take swings at him for an hour.

"At least Acksel listened to reason." She stroked her hand through Luke's hair as she sat next to him on the bed.

Dade snorted. "He behaved like a child. Anyone with half a brain would have known those idiots were hiding something. Acksel knew something was going on between you two and took the opportunity to use the pack to take out his frustrations."

Eveny told Luke that her dad had talked to other pack members and found out that her boss and Luke's boss had both been encouraged to keep them busy so they wouldn't have time to talk before her heat-cycle.

Luke had asked if they thought Acksel planned to have Vince go to her all along and they both agreed that it was the most likely scenario. Luke didn't particularly care what Acksel's reasoning was for sending Vince to Eveny, and he was glad that Vince was dead and the truth had come out.

"Do you think Acksel will lose his position?" Eveny asked her dad.

"Why would that happen?" Luke asked.

She smiled at him. "Because he let you go. A lot of wolves feel that humans are inferior and that pack members should be held in higher esteem. They know that I mated you. They watched me and my dad take you out of the chains at Acksel's direction and leave. Then he punished the three wolves."

Dade said, "Acksel told the pack that it was according to pack law, but it will be hard for many wolves to understand why he would change his mind like he did."

Dade straightened and opened the door. "I'm going to grab some boxes and head over to your place, Luke. We need to be ready to go in five days."

"Thank you." Luke said.

Dade said, "You're not picking an easy path, Luke, but we're a family now and family sticks together."

He shut the door behind them and Eveny turned on the bed to look at him. "What can I get you?"

"Another kiss would be great."

She chuckled and leaned forward, kissing the corner of his mouth. "You're insatiable."

"Just for you."

———————

By the morning of the fifth day, Luke was feeling less like he'd gotten run over by a truck and more like himself. He could see clearly out of both eyes now, and the doctor had given him a clean bill of health. Dade had packed up Luke's apartment several days earlier and brought everything over to the house, filling the garage with boxes. The apartment next to the bar had come furnished, so there was no furniture to move. His grandmother had visited every day and fussed over him and Eveny both, cooking, cleaning, and helping pack Eveny's and Dade's homes.

Luke looked into the garage and saw his life packed up in boxes. Eveny's arms went around his waist and she leaned on him. "You okay?" she asked, peering up at him.

"Yeah. I'm going to miss Wilde Creek, but I'm glad that I get to keep you."

She grinned. "I never thought I'd leave town, either, but it's better to go with you than stay and be alone and miserable."

He leaned down and kissed her. His lips were still healing, but he'd been unable to stop kissing her whenever the mood struck, which was often.

She sighed and rested her head against his chest, over his heart. He wished that things could be different. That they wouldn't have to leave town and live in a cabin. He'd broached the subject of finding another place to live besides the cabin, but realized quickly that they needed the safety of the woods around the cabin to hunt in their shift. Finding a new place to live required extensive research on their part, since they had to make sure that the place they chose to live was friendly towards shifters and had room to roam safely. Wilde Creek was a shifter-friendly town, but there were other places where shifters were not welcome.

The cabin was in the town of Potter, which was a tiny community that was friendly towards shifters, though not as friendly as Wilde Creek.

"You're giving up so much to be with me, Ev," he said quietly, holding her tightly against him.

"I'm happier to be leaving, Luke. Sure, Wilde Creek is nice, but the pack is stifling in its traditions. If I weren't leaving this year, it would be next year." She lifted her head to look at him. "I would have come back from my heat-cycle and told you that I wanted to be with you and we would have left anyway." She paused and then smiled. "Besides, I don't want our kids to grow up thinking that they can't love whoever they want. Only the inside of a person should matter, not whether they can shift or not."

"Kids?" He wiggled his brow.

"Oh yeah, lots." She winked and laughed, squeezing her arms tighter around his middle.

A loud engine rumbled and they turned to see Dade's truck, with a fifth-wheel camper attached, pull into the driveway with Dade behind the wheel.

"What's this, Dad?" Eveny asked when Dade got out.

"I borrowed it from a friend. I've ordered a trailer for myself, but it won't be delivered for a few weeks. The cabin is small enough as it is, so I'll stay in the camper."

Luke hadn't said anything before, but he'd wondered how he and Ev were going to find time to be together with her dad staying in the same one-room cabin. He breathed out a quiet sigh of relief and Eveny giggled.

"I heard that," she whispered.

Dade headed into the house and Luke looked down at her. "Can't help that I want to make love to you again, baby. And again and again."

"Are you sure you're well enough?"

He pressed her close as his cock sprang to life. "I'll never be too beat-up to make love to you."

Her hands flexed on his back and she growled lightly. "I'm so happy to be your mate, Luke."

"I'm happy to be yours, too, Eveny."

By the time they were ready to go to Acksel's house for the meeting, all of their belongings were loaded into Luke's truck and the fifth-wheel. They took Eveny's car to the meeting. Luke had very little memory of how he'd gotten to Acksel's the last time; he wasn't even sure who had knocked him out. He'd woken up as he was being chained to the pole and knew right away that Acksel had been lied to. His only worry had been that Eveny was safe, so he hadn't tried to defend himself by drawing her any further into the situation. Only once did he tell Acksel that he had the wrong information and was being lied to. He'd managed to stay conscious until Eveny showed up, and once he knew that she was safe, he'd let the darkness pull him down.

He was aware that if Eveny and Dade hadn't shown up when they did he most likely would have died chained up to a pole. The pack had been cheering for blood, calling for his death, and Acksel seemed all too happy to comply. Luke had never had a problem with Acksel before, but he had lost all respect for the male now and was glad to be taking Eveny away.

Acksel was standing on the back porch of his home and the pack was kneeling in a group several feet away. Luke gripped Eveny's hand tightly, ready to step in front of her at the slightest provocation.

Acksel's arms were folded across his chest and he regarded them silently as they came to stand in front of him, Eveny between himself and Dade.

His eyes narrowed and Eveny and Dade went to their knees. Eveny gripped his hand and pulled him down with her. He hadn't planned to kneel before the wolf, but he realized that he might make things intolerably worse for Eveny if he made a show of resisting. He'd never kneel before the bastard again, that was for damn sure.

Acksel looked at them for a long moment and then looked to the pack behind them. "An alpha cannot be a rod made of steel, unbending and unyielding to change. He must be willing to bend when he sees that the laws of old are choking the life from his pack."

Stillness settled over the yard and Luke looked at Acksel in confusion. Those didn't sound like the words of a man who was going to be sending his sister packing.

"As is my right as alpha, I declare that from this day forward, the members of the Wilde Creek pack may mate with whoever they choose, be they wolf, other supernatural creature, or human."

Acksel's voice rang out clearly and full of authority. Eveny gasped and Luke looked down at her. She glanced at him, but turned her attention back to her brother.

An angry murmur moved through the crowd and Acksel's voice rose over it. "Who speaks against their alpha?"

Two males stood up slowly and one said, "You cannot abandon the old ways because your sister is whoring with a human."

The other said, "Banish her and let us be free of the bad influence on our young."

Acksel moved so fast that Luke didn't even see him leave the porch. One minute he was standing calmly in front of them and the next minute he had the first wolf off the ground with his hand clasped around his neck. Blood poured from where Acksel's claws were digging into the male's skin.

"Call my sister a whore again and I'll rip your tongue out, Rever."

The second male crouched low behind Acksel and leapt at him, but Acksel tossed the first male aside and leaned into the other man. Their bodies hit with a loud sound and within seconds Acksel had the male pinned and twisted his arm behind his back until it cracked and the male howled.

Acksel stood slowly, blood dripping from his claws. He ripped his shirt off and howled. "I am alpha and my word is law! Defy me and know pain."

Eveny shivered next to Luke and he put his arm around her.

"What the hell is going on?" Luke said in a low voice.

Dade said, "Acksel is making a stand for Eveny."

"What does it mean?" he asked.

Eveny twisted her hand into Luke's shirt and hugged herself closer. "I don't know."

No one else challenged Acksel; every wolf bowed their head. "Our pack was built on blood," Acksel said, "but there is room for peace here. We live among humans, we can accept them as the mates of our members. You have until the next full moon to decide if you want to remain in the pack. Those that wish to leave will be allowed without fear of reprisal, but once the full moon has passed, the only way out of the pack is through banishment or death."

He dismissed the pack and walked through the yard, not stopping as he said, "Come inside," and continued on into the house.

Luke stood and helped Eveny to her feet, and the three of them followed Acksel into his house. He was watching out the kitchen window as the pack members cleared out. For several minutes, no one said anything, and then Acksel turned around and leaned against the counter.

"You were going to leave, Dad?"

"Yes. You didn't really leave me any choice."

Acksel's gray eyes darkened and he frowned and then he shook his head. "I know I've disappointed you, Dad, and I'm sorry. I've made a lot of mistakes over the last week and I owe all of you an apology."

Eveny wiped tears from her cheeks. "You broke my heart, Acksel, and you destroyed the trust between us."

Acksel looked like he might be sick.

Eveny paused for just a moment and then said, "But we're family, and although it's going to take me a long time to trust you again, you're my brother and I love you."

She left Luke's side to go to Acksel and hug him.

"I love you, too," Acksel hugged her and then looked at Luke. "I'm sorry. I wanted to keep you two apart because I didn't want to admit that the traditions of the pack were no longer valid. If I chose to ignore one tradition, then I needed to take a hard look at all of them."

Luke maybe didn't hate Acksel so much right now. "What's going to happen to the pack?"

Eveny moved away from Acksel and back into Luke's arms.

"I'm not sure. We'll lose some members, those that are truly against humans and wolves mating. Most of the pack are ambivalent. As long as I'm not going to allow humans to actually join the pack, then they won't really care what others do." He moved to the refrigerator and took out three beers and a bottle of apple juice, distributing them. "I want you to go ahead and buy the bar, Luke, if that's what you want. I promise that I'll continue to hold business meetings there and that nothing will change as far as the pack using it for a hang out. I would ask that you find a place to live away from the bar so you're not raising my niece or nephew in that kind of environment, if you don't mind."

Eveny grinned and took a drink of apple juice. "I think we can manage that."

"Good." Acksel drained the beer, crushing the can and tossing it into the trash. "If you want to stay in Wilde Creek with the pack, then I'm willing to accept Luke as your mate, Ev. As long as Luke understands that I'm your alpha and that you have responsibilities to the pack, then you're welcome to stay. I can't promise that I won't be a dick, but I promise to try not to be such a hard ass."

Eveny looked up at Luke. "It's up to you. I want to be wherever you are, because that's home for me."

Luke's heart melted just a little bit. "Then let's stay."

Even though he didn't believe that things would be easy if they stayed in Wilde Creek, he believed that Acksel had found a way to protect Eveny and their child, and to allow the pack to change with the times. If Acksel was willing to put his position of alpha on the line to let them stay in Wilde Creek, then Luke could be a big enough person to forgive what had happened and let it go.

"I think we have some unpacking to do," Luke leaned down and kissed Eveny's cheek.

"And house hunting," she smiled.

"You can stay at the garage apartment until you find a permanent place," Dade said. "Dinner's at five every night."

Luke, Eveny, and Dade left and headed back to Dade's home. As she and Luke walked up the stairs to her apartment, she said, "What should we do first? Unpack your stuff or mine?"

He opened the door for her and kicked it shut. "You've got ten seconds to get naked or I'm going to tear your clothes off."

Her mouth dropped open. "What?"

He gave her his most wicked grin. "One."

She shrieked in laughter and pulled her top off, racing towards the bedroom as Luke continued to count, leaving a trail of clothes behind him.

CHAPTER TWELVE

Acksel, sitting at his regular booth at Poke's, was halfway through a bottle of whiskey when Auro sat down. He was two years older than Acksel and had been a good friend. But seeing as how he had misjudged his other so-called friends and nearly gotten his sister killed, he wasn't putting too much faith in his ability to choose friends wisely.

"Are you looking for some company, or would you rather be alone?" Auro asked.

Acksel looked up. "Three families have already given notice that they won't be staying in the pack."

Auro raised a brow. "You're not surprised, are you? Some of the members are very pro-wolf and anti-human.

He swirled the whiskey in the glass and exhaled. "No, I guess I'm not."

"For what it's worth, Acksel, I would be sticking by you if I weren't leaving because of Melanie. I don't have a problem with humans. In fact, Mel's got a cousin that's mated to a human and they're accepted by their pack. I say to each their own, you know? Humans don't float my boat, but that doesn't mean I hate anyone that digs them."

"It's not that easy when you're alpha and you're responsible for upholding the traditions that have been in existence since our people were created."

Auro leaned his elbows on the table. "It's only difficult if you make it that way, Acksel. You're the alpha and you make the laws. If you say that humans can be mates to wolves and they're to be accepted, then that's what the law is."

"Someone could fight me." He pointed out.

Auro chuckled. "And you'll put them down. I don't think you're afraid of that. I think you're concerned about opening a floodgate. As if Eveny mating a human is going to make all the single wolves take human mates."

The thought had crossed Acksel's mind. "Humans and wolves only have a 50/50 chance of having a child that shifts. With each generation introducing humans into the equation, the odds go down that much further. In a few generations, there won't be any wolves born at all."

"We'll be dead and partying in the afterlife, man. If that's the natural order of things, then it is. You're worrying about something that you can't control. And although you're one fucking powerful alpha, even you can't control someone's destiny."

Acksel hummed in his throat and swallowed the rest of the whiskey. Reaching for the bottle, he filled up his glass and listened to Auro tell him about getting ready to leave with his mate.

With each glass of whiskey, his mood darkened and his chest tightened with grief. He couldn't stop reliving the moment when Eveny called him out on his behavior, asking if he was going to take her mate away. He'd seen it so clearly in her eyes — at that moment, she was choosing Luke. Acksel had never been in love. He'd been fucking random she-wolves who wanted to become his mate solely because he was alpha, but they didn't know anything about him. They didn't really care about him. Before this mess with Eveny, he hadn't cared about that. But now...it mattered. He wanted to be a male who mattered to a female. Someone who would worry if he was late getting home. Someone who wouldn't want anything from him but his love.

Tipping the bottle over, he watched a few drops splash into the glass and realized he had finished the whole bottle by himself. It took a lot to get him drunk, but a whole bottle of whiskey was making him very fuzzy around the edges. Auro had left...at some point, but he didn't remember when. The bar was still open, but the crowd had thinned out, which told him it was probably close to closing time.

Making his way out of the bar, he knew he was too toasted to drive, so he decided to walk instead of sleeping it off in his truck. Blinking a few times to clear his vision, he started off down the street towards his home.

Several streets later, a scent caught his nose and woke his whole body and mind up instantly. He paused on the sidewalk and inhaled slowly and deeply. He smelled a scent that was so familiar and made his body warm and his cock harden. He followed the scent, wondering what it was that smelled so good and made his wolf pant and growl in his mind.

Turning up a stone walkway, he paused and inhaled again. Cinnamon.

He stumbled up the stone front steps and smashed into the front door. Leaning his cheek against the cool wood, he began to knock.

A voice that he recognized but couldn't place came through the door. "Who is it?"

"Open up. I want to see you," he growled, his wolf whining plaintively in his mind.

He had to know who belonged to the intoxicating scent.

"Acksel?" A bright light over the door blinded him momentarily and he shielded his eyes and leaned back as the door opened.

He leaned heavily on the door jam and stared at the woman who had opened the door. She was beautiful. And she smelled like cinnamon, and something else.

He inhaled deeply and growled. Oh yes, she smelled like she belonged to him.

Darkness edged his vision and the woman gasped and reached for him. "Acksel? Are you okay?"

"I just want someone to care," he mumbled as he went to his knees and then slumped to the ground.

Soft, warm fingers touched his forehead and the scent of cinnamon filled his nose. "I always cared, Acksel," the woman whispered and he slipped off into darkness, praying he wasn't dreaming.

CHAPTER THIRTEEN

Eveny unpacked the last box of kitchen items in their new home and stretched the kink out of her back. She'd been on her feet all evening, trying to unpack as much as she could while Luke was at the bar. He'd made her swear not to be on her feet too much, but she didn't want to sit on her butt while he did everything.

Every day after work for the last week, she came home and Luke was waiting with dinner for her. They ate together and talked, and then he left for his shift. She didn't like working opposite shifts, but she was glad that she could spend some time with him.

It had been almost two weeks since Acksel had declared that they could stay in town. The full moon was tomorrow night, and she was anxious to see her brother. He'd been acting strange lately, and she didn't think it was just that he was concerned about how many people were going to leave before the full moon, or that someone would challenge his position as alpha.

Her phone rang and she answered it.

"You're not unpacking, are you, Ev?" Luke asked.

"What are you, psychic?" She laughed.

"No," he chuckled, "I just know my mate. You promised you wouldn't work too hard and I have a feeling that you started unpacking as soon as I left."

Maybe he really was psychic. "I'll stop. I finished the kitchen, and that was what I really wanted to do, anyway. We ate soup out of coffee mugs tonight because we couldn't find the bowls."

"It's rustic."

"It's lazy." She leaned against the counter. "I think I'm going to unpack one more box, though."

"You should be relaxing, baby."

"Oh, I will. After."

"After what?"

"After I find the box of my sex toys."

There was a long pause and then he said in a low voice, "Why the hell would you need to find those?"

She grinned to herself. Teasing him was so much fun. "Because I'm horny and alone. Too bad my mate isn't home right now to help me out."

She heard hurried movements on his end and she stifled a laugh. He covered the receiver but she still heard him say, "I'm cutting out early, Eveny needs me at home."

"I don't need you," she said with a laugh. "I have toys."

"Don't fucking start without me, Ev," he said roughly, and she heard his truck door open and close forcefully.

"Better be quick, Luke," she whispered and ended the call, grinning when he called her right back. She ignored it, knowing it would drive him nuts. She only had a few minutes before he got home, so she put the empty box outside on the back porch for the trash and hurried to the bedroom, stripping her clothes off.

The home they were renting was close to the bar in a quiet neighborhood on a tree-lined street. The yard butted up against a stretch of pine trees and she loved to sit out on the back patio at night and watch the stars and listen to the birds and animals settle down for bed. The small ranch home was perfect for them, with three bedrooms, a quaint kitchen, and a stone fireplace that conjured images of cold winter nights in front of it with Luke's arms around her.

She brushed her teeth and checked out her reflection in the mirror, pressing her hand to her stomach lightly. She was a few weeks along and wasn't showing, but she couldn't help but feel like everyone could tell she was pregnant because she was smiling so much. She never expected the idea of motherhood and being mated to fill her with such joy.

Their mating night — the night that created this child — had been filled with so many emotions, chief of which had been her fear that Luke might die trying to keep her safe. But he hadn't died, and they were a family now and she was still part of the pack. Luke's potential sacrifice had done much more than save her from being raped...it had changed one of the core beliefs of her pack and allowed her to stay with him without losing her pack, dad, and brother.

She heard the sound of Luke's truck as it pulled quickly into the driveway, and she smiled at her reflection in the mirror before turning off the light and walking to the bed.

Easing herself up onto the mattress, she leaned back on her elbows and crossed her legs, dangling her feet off the end. Luke stomped through the house, making a growling sound that she found so sexy. She wasn't sure he was even aware that he made that sound when he was turned on, but the rumbling sound from his throat made her whole body light up.

He entered the bedroom and exhaled loudly as he tore his plain white tee off. "No toys?"

She smiled. "Why would I use toys when your fingers and tongue set my world on fire?"

"If I hadn't come home?" He moved in front of her and undid the button of his jeans.

"I would have been thinking of you," she promised, laughing when he bared his teeth in displeasure. "You've been hanging around wolves too much, Luke. You're picking up all our bad habits."

He shoved his jeans down his legs and divested himself of the rest of his clothes. Gripping his thick cock, he stroked it from base to tip and grinned wickedly. "You want this, baby?"

She parted her legs and stretched out on her back, gripping the blanket above her head. "You know I do."

His eyes darkened. He gripped her knees with his hands and pulled her closer to the end of the bed, his cock just inches away from her pussy. With one smooth thrust, he entered her, burying himself deeply inside her. Her toes curled at the heat that filled her as he pressed as closely to her as he could, his hands tightening on her knees. His hips shifted and he eased out of her, holding her gaze as he pushed back inside faster.

She hooked her ankles around his back and he released her knees, leaning over her and planting his hands on the bed as he began to thrust into her in a fast rhythm. His hands gripped the blanket covering the bed and his knuckles turned white with the strain as he drove into her again and again.

His hands slipped underneath her body and he gripped her shoulders, pulling her down to meet his thrusts. Their bodies slammed together, driving the breath from her lungs, as the angle of his body rubbed her clit just right. Her belly tightened and she released her hold on the blanket and dug her nails into his shoulders, moaning his name as her climax reached a pinnacle and she fell off the edge into white-hot pleasure.

She cried out as she came, her body writhing under his as her nerve endings went haywire and her pussy clutched his cock. He let out a gusty breath as he came, burying his face in her neck as he shuddered.

Tracing the line of his spine, she kissed his cheek and sighed in bliss. "You're so much better than a toy, Luke."

He chuckled and nipped at her neck with his teeth. "I'm glad you think so, baby, but let's keep the toy-to-man comparisons to ourselves, okay? I don't need anyone in your pack knowing that there's a box full of my competition in this house."

She crossed her heart with her fingers. "Promise."

He angled off her with a grunt and patted her thigh. "Up on your hands and knees, Ev."

She blinked in surprise and he wiggled his brows. "I've got the night off work and you said you were horny, which makes me horny just thinking about it. So yeah, sweetness, we're not done yet. Not by a long shot."

She couldn't stop from smiling. "Promise?"

"Promise." He eased away from her and watched as she wiggled around on the bed until she was on her hands and knees. He joined her, sliding his hands up the backs of her thighs and teasing the seam of her sex. "Love you, Ev."

"I love you, too," she said, her voice trailing off in a moan as they made love once more. And then once more after that.

And then another time before the morning light bathed the bedroom in peach and gold.

As she drifted off to sleep in Luke's arms, she thanked her lucky stars that she'd been fortunate enough to have her best friend as her mate. She knew that no matter what happened to them in the future, Luke would stand beside her. No matter the danger or the odds against him. There was no one else more perfect for her than Luke, the mate of her heart.

The End

———·———

Contact the Author

Website: http://www.rebutlerauthor.com
Email: rebutlerauthor@gmail.com
Twitter: @rebutlerauthor
Facebook: www.facebook.com/R.E.ButlerAuthorPage

Also from R. E. Butler

Wiccan-Were-Bear Novella Series
A Curve of Claw
A Flash of Fang
A Price for a Princess
A Bond of Brothers
A Bead of Blood
A Twitch of Tail

The Wolf's Mate Series
The Wolf's Mate Book 1: Jason & Cadence
The Wolf's Mate Book 2: Linus & The Angel
The Wolf's Mate Book 3: Callie & The Cats
The Wolf's Mate Book 4: Michael & Shyne
The Wolf's Mate Book 5: Bo & Reika
The Wolf's Mate Book 6: Logan & Jenna

The Necklace Chronicles
The Tribe's Bride
The Gigolo's Bride

Ashland Pride Series
Seducing Samantha (Ashland Pride One)
Loving Lachlyn (Ashland Pride Two)

Hyena Heat Series
Every Night Forever (Hyena Heat One)
Every Dawn Forever (Hyena Heat Two)

Wilde Creek
Mate of Her Heart

———•———

Coming Soon...The Alpha's Heart (Wilde Creek Book Two)

Alpha wolf Acksel wakes up one morning in the bed of a woman he's had a crush on since high school. Brynn Mara was the one human who had been friendly to him in school and now, ten years later, she is snuggled up at his side, smelling like passion and sweet dreams. Even though Acksel has declared that his pack members can mate with humans from now on, he knows that any woman he takes as his mate will have a target on her back. Especially if she's a fragile human. Deciding it's better to cut things off than string her along when there is no hope for a relationship, he leaves without a word and ignores her.

But it doesn't matter if Acksel acknowledges her or not, because their one night of passion has left a permanent reminder of what happens when one drunk wolf forgets protection. Angry, banished wolves from his pack discover Brynn's secret and decide to use her against Acksel. His worst fears have come true and the only woman that ever touched his heart is now suffering because of his mistake. Can he save her in time?

This book contains one pissed-off, emotionally damaged alpha, the human woman who can tame him, and a sweet little surprise that no one expected.

—·—